TURBULENCE

TURBULENCE

a novel

Chico Buarque

Translated from the Portuguese by Peter Bush

Pantheon Books • New York

All rights reserved under International and Pan-American Copyright Conventions. Published in the United States by Pantheon Books, a division of Random House, Inc., New York. Originally published in Brazil as *Estorvo* by Companhia Das Letras, São Paulo, in 1991. Copyright © 1991 by Chico Buarque. This translation originally published in Great Britain by Bloomsbury Publishing Ltd., London, in 1992.

Library of Congress
Cataloging-in-Publication Data

Buarque de Hollanda, Chico, 1944–
[Estorvo. English]
Turbulence : a novel / Chico Buarque :
translated from the Portuguese by Peter Bush.
p. cm.
Translation of: Estorvo.
ISBN 0-679-41264-6
I. Title.
PQ9698.18.O35E7713 1992
869.3—dc20   91-50837

Book design by Guenet Abraham

Manufactured in the United States of America

First American Edition

turbulence, disturbance, perturb,
intrude, twirl, swirl, stir,
extirpate, turbid, stupor,
torpor, tremor, thunder,
tumult, multitude, mutilate,
mutable, trouble, turmoil,
turbulence

TURBULENCE

ONE

It's very early for me, I went to bed in broad daylight, can't make out that fellow through the spyhole. I'm dizzy, can't understand the fellow standing there in a suit and tie, with his face swollen by the lens. It must be something important, I heard the bell ring several times, once on my way to the door and at least three times in my sleep. My eyes are focusing now and I'm starting to think I knew that face in a distant, hazy past. Or was I asleep when I got to the spy-hole, do I know that face from when it was still part of my dreams? It's got a beard. Perhaps I have seen that face before without a beard, but the beard's so solid and exact, as if it came before the face. The suit and tie also unsettle me. I don't know many people who wear suits and ties, much less with hair hanging down to their shoulders. The suit-and-tie individuals I know live behind desks and ticket windows, they're not individuals who come hammering on my door. I try to imagine the man clean-shaven and in shirt-sleeves, allow for the distortions of the spy-hole, but he's still someone I know and can't put a name to. And the static close-ups of the fellow's face confuse my judgement even more. It's not exactly a face, more the image of a face that gets farther from the real face the better you know the individual. For me, that immobility is his best disguise.

I retreat cautiously across my flat as if moving through water. I'll slip back into bed, I think the fellow will give up in the end, now he's sure nobody is at home. But I'm just crossing the imaginary line between my bedroom and living room when the bell rings again. I can't sleep with the image of that man attached to my door. I go back to the spy-hole. I must catch one careless, impatient movement that will give him away, enable me to link the gesture to the person. And while I'm there, he doesn't ring the bell, look at his watch, light a cigarette, or take his eye away from the spy-hole. Now I realise he's watching me the whole time. Through the spy-hole in reverse, he sees me as a concave man. That's how he saw me come and try to decipher him with an eye glued to the hole, saw me move away in slow motion, in long strides, saw me turn round looking contorted, and saw me seeing him, knowing me better than I know him. Because I only sense that he isn't what he pretends to be, a salesman, a manager, a zombie. And he knows me well enough to know I might even welcome a stranger in, but would never open my door to someone who really wanted to come in.

Now he knows it's useless, that he doesn't fool me any more, I won't open up, that I could die there without a murmur, turn into a skeleton standing right opposite his skeleton, so he shakes his head and leaves my field of vision. And that last glimpse gives me all I need to identify him fully, and then immediately forget him. I just know it was someone who was with me a long time ago, but whom I shouldn't have seen, whom I didn't need to see again, because he was someone who one day shook his head and left my field of vision, a long time ago.

That's an end to sleep. From my sixth-floor window I can observe the pavement in front of the building. The man soon comes out, stops on the kerb but doesn't look up at my window, as I would have in his place. After such a long wait in my corridor, he should risk a last glance. Anyone else would look up at the sixth floor, even knowing it was useless; they would look to check there wasn't a light on, that there wasn't a towel over the windowsill, would automatically look, a knee-jerk kind of hope. They would only not look if they knew they were being watched. He knows I'm watching him call a taxi, settle in the front seat and tell the driver to take the first right. I put my clothes on quickly, reckoning that right now he'll be stuck at the red light on the next corner. Reckoning I'm putting my clothes on quickly, he'll tell the driver to jump the light and turn right once, twice, a third time. He'll complete the tour of the block predicting I'm in the lift, with my shirt still flapping. But I button up by the window watching his taxi complete its drive round the block.

He'll be leaping from his taxi as I definitively slam my door shut, his driver calling him a bastard after such a stupid run-around. He'll be disappointed at not bumping into me in the lobby. He'll ask the porter about me, and I'm between the fifth and fourth floors, walking down slowly because the lights fused. The porter's listening to the radio and will reply he doesn't know the business of anyone in the building. As I reach the second floor, he'll get into the lift, after prodding the button forty times. Near ground-level I come across the light from the street that flashes up the front of the stairs. On the last stretch of this twisted staircase I miss my step; I step into the light and fly headlong across the lobby, and he's in my corridor. Now he won't ring the bell; he'll smash the lock, with me on the pavement opposite.

I don't need to look at the sixth floor to know he's spying on me from my own window. He'll see me hurry and disappear up the first turning on the left. And he'll call the lift and he'll call a taxi but he won't persuade the driver to chase me the wrong way up a one-way street. He'll take a parallel street, as I head down the tunnel, reach another district, breathe new smells. He'll be stuck in traffic as I climb the hills, past terraces of forest, invisible slopes with invisible mansions from where one can survey the whole city.

.   .   .

The guard in the fortified sentry-box is a new member of staff, and it's his duty to keep me out of the condominium. He asks me who I am and where I'm going, his eyes on my shoes. He calls number 16 on the intercom to say there's a gentleman here who says he's brother to the lady of the house. Number 16 says something in reply that the guard doesn't like and he goes "Mmm." The gate with its green iron bars and gilt knobs judders open as if reluctant to let me in. The guard watches me walk up the slope, scrutinises the soles of my shoes, and thinks to himself that I'm the first pedestrian authorised to pass through that gate. Number 16, at the end of the condominium, has got another intercom, another electronic gate and two armed security guards. The dogs bark in unison, then suddenly stop. A lad holding a cleaning rag opens the side door and waves me into the garden.

My sister's house is a glass pyramid that has no apex. A steel frame supports the four sides, which are made of trapezoid-shaped panes of reinforced glass, either as fixed panes, or doors or tilting windows. The few brick-built inside walls were conceived so that anyone coming into the garden would be able to look through the house to the ocean and the islands beyond. However, later on, to keep the rooms cool, white, black, blue, red and yellow curtains were hung everywhere, a huge, abstract panel in place of the horizon. The circular patio in the belly of the house also originally sheltered a fig tree, the branches of which emerged from the top of the frustrated pyramid. It turned out that, when the house was ready, it began to stifle the fig tree, whose roots counter-attacked by undermining the foundations. Architect and landscape designer were summoned in, harangued each other, till it became obvious that house and fig tree would never coexist.

I always thought that prize-winning piece of architecture would prefer life in some other place. The house freed itself of the fig tree, but still doesn't seem satisfied with the land it's on, the garden that's all around, the slime sticking to its concrete supports, the ivy clinging to its panes of glass. In this dispute the gardener has taken pity on the house, and spends his days pulling the ivy off, polishing the concrete, pruning whatever strikes him. One day, beside himself in anger, he turned the flower beds upside down, eliminated the hydrangeas, and would have reduced the garden to a golf course had my sister not intervened. As she has studied at the Botanical Gardens, my sister likes to walk through the grove along the side of the house, being able to tell an *ipê* from a *carvalho*, an *oiticica*, a *jequitibá* or a *maçaranduba*. She also looks after the palm trees that line up separately, ever since she found out that palm trees belong to a haughty race that in turn is scorned by serious trees. And when my sister has time, she goes to the far corners of the grounds to the wall where the garden meets the woods; she only walks back at twilight, stopping to watch and listen to the play of the foliage, along paths even the gardener is unaware of. But today, with the sun high in the sky and not a hint of breeze, my sister is inside and the foliage is not at play; each leaf is a model leaf, with its dark-green in the light and light-green in the shade. Today it looks like the garden is studying architecture.

The servant can't decide which door to the house I deserve, since I'm not here to deliver nor do I look like a visitor. He pauses, wrings the rag to squeeze out his doubts, and opts for the garage door, which is neither here nor there. I obey the convulsed signals from his rag and walk round the cars in the transparent garage, up the spiral staircase, and enter a kind of living room with an unusually high ceiling, a granite floor, a tilted glass wall, other bare, white walls, a lot of echo, a living room where I never saw anyone sit down. On the left of this room is a large staircase which leads to the second floor. And at the foot of that staircase is a small room they call the winter garden, next to the inside patio where the fig tree used to live. And here is my sister in her dressing-gown, drinking morning coffee at an oval table.

She twitches her eyebrows in my direction, then looks down again so her hair falls over her face, absorbed in the photos she is sifting into small heaps. They set out a place for me opposite her, some distance away, and she doesn't look up but passes me photos where there are no people, only parks, streets, snow, repeated landscapes I dispatch in half a minute. They must be photos from the beginning of her trip, when she was lonely and emotionally drained; though she's studied photography, her framing is uneven, she under- or over-exposed, as if she was in a rush to finish the film. In the photos she's piling up out of my reach I imagine her now with a fresh complexion, perhaps she's opening her arms on a bridge, having shown a stranger how to handle the camera. And in the more recent photos she's standing behind the milk jug, I expect there are the friends she keeps making, and the friends of friends, and artists and public figures, and the lights of the boat during the farewell dinner.

The butler comes in with a tray from the kitchen, not that I heard my sister ring for him, and he picks up the different heaps of photos one by one. I was going to ask to see the complete set, but my sister looks up and asks if I've visited Mummy. She says Mummy has been so lonely, she doesn't even want a servant, she only has a cleaner who goes every Tuesday and Thursday, but Mummy doesn't think a cleaner is company. The ideal would be to take on a nurse, but Mummy thinks a nurse soon gets over-friendly, and any moment Mummy may have a fall, because her eyesight is getting worse and worse. As she talks, my sister spreads a film of purple jam over her toast, as if she is enamelling the toast, then she takes stock, puts aside the purple jam and finishes off with the orange; she goes to take a bite, changes her mind, has a sip of tea and marvels at how people can grow old overnight, for when Father died people thought Mummy would go downhill, not a bit of it, she gathered steam, went to the theatre, dined out, enjoyed horse-riding on the farm, simply adored the farm, drank her drop of whisky, played tennis, damn

it, to think that only last year Mummy was still playing tennis.

Their little girl rushes past me and hurls herself
round her mother's neck. She's wearing school uniform, a lunch-box strapped on her back and double
plaits. My sister pinches her on the cheeks, sits her
on her knees and jogs her up and down, tickles her
under her arms, rubs noses Indian-style and gives
her the one-eyed Martian treatment. They stay nose
to nose for hours on end, each one wanting to be the
other. The girl says "That's enough," jumps over the
floor, advances on the cream crackers and by chance
notices my presence. My sister asks her if she's
going to say hello to her uncle. She stretches out her
arms towards me as if she wants a hug, but suddenly
transforms her hands into two pistols, comes at me
and almost perforates my eyes. Then she lets out a
dry, guttural laugh that's quite unchildlike; her
whole body starts to shake and she forces the laughter out till she is breathless, then recovers with an
asthmatic gasp, and starts up a new laugh, gasping
and choking, shaking and laughing till she turns
blue. The nanny comes and takes the girl away.

My sister lays the clean cutlery on the plate with
the toast, and I know it's the time she usually gets
dressed to go out. I expect her chauffeur is now at

the ready, map in hand, to take her wherever she orders, and every day she orders him to a different place. Today she may announce the name of a district on the other side of the city, and when they get there she'll say "I think that's it," or "It's the next turning," or "We've gone past," making it clear once again that she's making the address up. Perhaps she'll order her chauffeur to wait in front of a yellow boarding-house where she'll spend four hours, looking more spruce on the way out than on the way in and anxious to get home, in the rush hour. Perhaps she'll arrive at the same time as her husband, and the two chauffeurs will drive side by side up the slope to the condominium. She may go with her husband up to their bedroom, and, as she sheds her clothes, may say she spent four hours in a yellow boarding-house in a commuter-town, but I don't know if her husband will believe her or pay any attention. I don't know if her husband will sit on the bed and loosen his belt, and ask her to stay just the way she is, with her hands in her hair. Nor do I know if her husband knows she gives me money from time to time. I didn't notice my sister call the butler who now brings a cheque book and silver pen on a tray.

She writes out the cheque, and her chestnut-brown hair doesn't enable me to see if she's really smiling, not even if that smile means I'm a no-hoper. The careless signature, together with the smile I can't see, means she won't miss the money. The tearing noise of the cheque being ripped out may mean this is the last time. But the way she conceals and places the cheque by my saucer, as if dealing a good card, and slides her palm away, caressing the tablecloth, as if she were erasing something, and saying "Forget it," means I can count on her whenever I want. She gets up, says she's running late, adding "Stay as long as you want," she doesn't know whether to smile, and wets her lips with her tongue, tidies her hair behind her ear and goes.

My sister walks in a single, clear movement. Her body seems to do nothing, her body ceases to exist, and beneath the silk dressing-gown there's only movement. A movement creating the shape of a body beneath the silk dressing-gown. And I wonder, as she climbs the stairs, if it isn't a body disguised that way which hands desire most to touch, not to encounter the flesh, but dreaming of fingering the movement itself. Some women are very aware of these things. But are they aware all the time? At any hour of the day? In any situation? In front of anyone? And suddenly my sister turns round at the top of the stairs, so suddenly as if to take me by surprise, as if she wanted to know whether I was looking at her and how. My sister spins round on the stairs just to remind me: "Don't forget Mummy."

I'm off-balance, alone at the oval table, looking at the honey, the goat's cheese, the rosehip tea, thinking about my mother. The butler brings a cordless telephone on a tray; a gadget with minute numbers, which I dial very quickly, almost wanting to hit the other numbers. I hear the phone ring once, twice, five times, the phone in an old person's house. Mummy picks it up but says nothing, she never says anything, because she considers it vulgar for a woman to say hello. I say "Mummy," and can feel her put the phone next to her ear, to stop her left hand from shaking. The butler pushes the trolley in, asks "Have you finished?" and takes the plates without stacking them. I repeat "Mummy," but I haven't got a lot to say, and the butler screws up the canoe-shaped napkin which I'd left untouched in front of me. Mummy can't have realised it was me and soon after the line goes dead. The butler scrapes a kind of spatula over the sky-blue tablecloth to collect up the cream-cracker crumbs, as I mouth a few words into the telephone.

TWO

I get to the bus station, with a tidy sum in each trouser pocket, four bundles of small notes the bank cashier got it into his head to give me for my cheque. My trousers fit tight, show off the bulges. I find an empty lavatory and separate out the money for my ticket. The man behind the desk examines each note front and back, though they're not very old or even that new. Ticket in hand I walk from bay to bay trying not to stand out. I cut a path through the

crowd, but always seem to bump into the same people. They seem equally surprised to keep seeing me
walk by. Back in the lavatory, I lock the door and
wait for the bus.

Better not to doze off on this bus. A thin character
in a check shirt sits down next to me; I'd already
seen him leaning against a stone upright. We're
shoulder to shoulder on the same seat, and I can't
see his face properly. I can see his hands, but
they're just like any other man's hands, a pair of
dirty, clasped hands. Except that now and then he
opens out the fingers of his right hand one by one, as
if he's adding up, to clench them all at once. The
next instant he opens out the whole hand and
clenches his fingers one at a time, now doing his
sums in reverse order. He's wearing open-toed sandals, and rubs his big toe over nearby toe-joints, like
someone counting money with their feet. He's not
carrying a suitcase, bag, or briefcase, a newspaper
or comic, doesn't look like a traveller; then it's
hardly a journey, this hour and a quarter of bends
and slopes to Brialuz service station where I'll jump
off. I excuse myself, and he has to get up to let me
by. I say "Brialuz service station" to the driver, and
as the bus brakes the checkered character stumbles

down the aisle, almost knocks me over. I get off the bus, he's behind. I take four steps over the verge and swing my body round, much as I saw my sister do. But the character was already across the road and walking up the slope that leads off elsewhere.

It upsets me to find the gate to the farm open. I think of the entrances to the condominium, and for a moment that wide-open gate is more impenetrable. I feel that, when I walk through the gateway, I won't be going in somewhere, but I'll be leaving every other place behind. Now I can see the whole valley and its boundaries, even so, it's as if the valley enclosed the world and now I was off into the outside. After this stupid hesitation, I realise that's just what I want. I step on the farmland, and I'm off. I step on the farmland, and, to feel secure, decide to shut the gate behind me. Except it's stuck in the ground, encrusted and embedded in dry mud. When I left the farm for the last time five years ago, I must have left the gate open and nobody ever came to close it.

For five years I abandoned and forgot all about this. Perhaps the inertia of the farm in my mind, rather than the long drought, accounts for this harsh light and the flat landscape. After overcoming the gate, I'm not sure of my way in. Maybe the breach is the night rising up from the bottom of the valley. The sun's still on the mountain tops, while night climbs up the slopes like crude oil. I sit down on the round stone where I sat when I was small, when I used to think that night first filled up the valley, then overflowed into earth and heaven.

When night closes perfectly around me, no moon or stars, no delights, nothing at all, I jump up from the stone and walk down the dirt track into the farm. The track leads straight to a stream, which it then criss-crosses. But I don't hear the stream. To tell the truth, I don't know whether I'm walking on beaten earth or through vegetation. I've not lost my way on the farm, more likely the undergrowth has invaded the path, or the stream has evaporated. But music keeps putting me off course. I accept this reluctantly, for there never used to be music on the farm; now there is music, lots of music filling every space with that substance music possesses in the dark. Music almost grazing me, as I reach the plank bridge over the stream.

I cross the bridge and on the other bank you only hear the stream, the water absorbs the music. A

small light is flickering in the main farmhouse, but I
don't need it to reach the eye of the valley, where I
thought night was born. Not far from my destination
I hear the first snarl. In this wilderness where I find
myself, I can only escape towards the house, and the
growing noise of barking makes me feel I'm running
towards the dogs. Because I'm fleeing in reverse, I
feel twice as fast; I imagine splitting the pack, like
two trains going opposite ways. I throw myself
against the front door that is bolted on the inside. I
go round the verandah, and the dogs quieten down
the moment I invade the kitchen.

The old man sitting on the stool strains in an effort
to lift up his head, just long enough for me to recognise our old caretaker. He's let his hair grow which,
white roots apart, looks as if it was just dipped into
a bucket of tar. The skin on his face seems paler,
more wrinkled than it used to be, and he's looking at
me questioningly, in a way I can't make out; perhaps
he's wondering who I am, perhaps he's wondering
whether I think the tint suits him. I almost slap him
on the back and say "Long time no see, old fellow,"
but such intimacy would strike false. My father
would burst in, roar with laughter in the old man's
face, run his hand through that greasy hair, even

kick the stool over and say, "Get up, you crook!" My father had a talent for shouting at his workers; he used to swear, throw them out on the street, call them back, sack them again, and they all came to his funeral. If I say "Long time no see, old fellow," it may be insulting because it's a different language.

Suddenly the old man springs toad-like into the middle of the kitchen, and points at me. He's wearing shorts held up by string beneath the waist; his ashen legs are still muscular, his shins slender; it's as if he belonged to a mixed race that grew old unevenly. He swings towards me like an acrobat, but hollow-chested, limp-armed, double-chinned, his thick-lipped mouth disclosing three teeth, his blue eyes bleary. He hugs me, kisses me, steps back, stands staring at me like a blind man, not into my eyes, but around my face, as if in search of my aura. "God bless you, God bless you," he says. Then asks "What happened to Osbenio? And to Clauir?" I realise he was expecting someone else, a relative, someone or other.

A bunch of green bananas on the kitchen floor reminds me that I've only had tea and biscuits. In the fridge, squat and open at the top, I find a jug of water, a pan of rice and a bowl of guava in syrup. I sit down with the bowl at the table where the employees used to eat. The old man guesses that I intend spending some time on the farm and gets all emotional again. He slumps down on the chair next to me, his eyes bleary this time with bitter tears. The old man tells me how his wife died two years ago, how he's in a bad way, and how the world swallowed up his children. He covers one nostril in order to blow the other, and says he's only got the kids left. Those other people, the outsiders, started to come and take over everything, the barn, the caretaker's house, the visitors' house, and took on strange people, knocked the stable down and ate the horses. And these others, the outsiders, are only waiting for him to die before taking possession of the house, that's why he sleeps in the pantry, why his grandchildren are spread round the living room and the bedrooms. He says the owners never come but when they do show up there'll be hell to pay.

I put a wad of notes on the table so the old man can stock up, but before I can explain myself, he pulls out a rucksack from under the table, throws the money inside and says "What's this for?" He puts the rucksack down, picks up a bottle of Underberg, says "With your permission," takes one gulp

and offers me the bottle complete with spittle round
the neck. He jumps up again and says "I'm going to
tidy up your bedroom." He runs through the house
and straight into the room that was always mine.

I should have let the old man clear out the kids.
When I go in the bedroom, the boy and the girl are
wide awake squatting on the mat in front of the television set. The kid, a seven-year-old with a shaven
head, looks but doesn't see me and returns to the
video-game control. The girl, an eight- or nine-year-
old, her thick, frizzy hair brushed to one side,
smiles, and keeps on smiling at me. I rip off my
clothes, stiff with dry sweat, and stretch out in my
underpants on the bare straw mattress on the bed
that was always mine. The old man had brought the
kids a thin striped mattress that belonged to the
lounger by the swimming pool.

I didn't bother about the children because I
thought I would lie down and sleep, but my eyelashes flicker with the flashing video game. On the
screen an intestine-like shape is pulsating, as little
green animals run down its tubes. For some reason,
these tubes sometimes get blocked, forcing the

shaven-headed kid into contortions with the control in his hands. Then the little animals crash together, knocking each other along like billiard balls, going bleep-bleep. Sometimes they also get stuck against the sides of the tube, in a chain reaction that causes the intestine to explode, to alarm bells and dazzling lights. The little animals float across the white screen and the game begins time and again, but after a while the girl with the head of hair, who was urging her brother on, gives a deep yawn and gets up. I watch her move from television to mattress, skirt the bed, skirt me, stop, turn round to pick up an elastic band, and against the light it's an adolescent swaying between my eyelashes. She stares at me, and her face is at most a ten-year-old's, to judge by the two front teeth still embedded in her gums, the impossible-to-comb hair, and the runny nose. Yet the small body walks along like a mature woman, choosing each step according to bodily criteria, and so she walks with pride rather than purpose, in a knee-length T-shirt that proclaims "Only Jesus Saves."

The straw irritating my skin, the sweet guava in the pit of my stomach, the bodily discomforts are only insomnia's alibi. Real insomnia begins when the body is asleep. Half-damaged, the brain doesn't flow

with good ideas, is unable to resist, say, the return
of the man in the spy-hole, who may be a friend I've
lost track of, now come to talk about past business
and who couldn't stand my indifference, and who, in
a dream, would pull off his own beard in despair and
would be chinless, turning landlord who had come
for the rent. But this is no dream and I owe the
landlord nothing, since my sister has backed me,
advanced six months' rent as a deposit, and, when
Mummy dies, my share in the inheritance won't pay
what I owe sis, so she may have given my address to
a lawyer, a legal officer, a bearded notary in the spy-
hole. I'm just about to enter the dream when I remember it's my ex-wife who's got my address; I left
a message in her house, a formal note, or rather an
ironic communiqué, or rather a curt rejoinder, and
anyway my ex-wife wouldn't write down my address
in her diary, what for? To give it to the man in the
spy-hole who may be her boyfriend, and I imagine
that man in suit and tie and beard in bed with my ex-
wife. What could a boyfriend of hers want from me?
Advice? An allowance? Confidences? Satisfaction?
Retrospective jealousy? My sister's sleek-haired Ar-
gentinian lover, brown suit and tie, swinging round
on the top of the stairs with my ex-wife? Soon, the

thoughts piling into my head settle down, more or less slot together, and it's a relief when thoughts stop chafing, and my head's sealed, tightening itself up, looking hollow on the outside. Sleep arrives like a boat from behind, and to sail away you must be unaware, for once you look at the boat, you miss your ride, go into a dry fall, drop down where you already are. And the shaven-headed kid is still sniffling and playing the video game. And the girl with the head of hair is still staring and smiling at me. And dawn has yet to break.

Now the girl gets up from the mattress, sways slowly towards me, this kid wants to lie with me, she kneels down, puts her face next to mine, is going to kiss me, thinks I'm sleeping, runs her breath right down over my body, goes to the foot of my bed, picks up my trousers and empties out the pockets. I want to react but can't, my body is dormant, my brain, my mouth can't let out a "Hey." The girl with the head of hair nudges her brother and they both run out.

My bedroom window looks out on the verandah, and I feel I've been asleep at a race-track. Through the wooden shutters I count twenty young kids cavorting and shouting under my window. A red motor bike roars in behind the house, cuts across the yard, climbs the slope opposite, and curves round with the machine almost horizontal. It dives down the slope, and no sooner is it round the left side of the house than it reappears on the right. Sparks fly off the cement in the yard, the bike climbs the slope, curves round, dives, and comes so quickly this time it's already shown up on one side before it's vanished from another. To complete its circuit, the bike flashes over the cement, attacks the slope and carries on, almost taking off before it hits the flat. Immediately surging back behind the house, it overreaches the slope with its wheels in the air and comes to rest against the bike that's waiting on the flat, because there are two of these red machines.

Now the old caretaker rushes into the yard carrying a glass of Underberg and whistles at the bikes through two fingers in his mouth. The kids laugh, clap and hurl limes at the old man. One of the two bikes points at him and accelerates down the slope. He raises his glass, puts his other hand over his face, bending so that the bike seems to cut through him without knocking him or his glass over. The rush of the wind spins his body ninety degrees, and it stops opposite the second bike that drives round the pool before hurtling down and across. The old man lurches, and this lurch is his salvation, for the bike is going so fast that swerving or braking is impossible. The kids shout "Olé!" and run over to the yard to cheer the old man, who drinks his Underberg, cross-legged.

I don't know what makes me jump through the window and go after the kids. By the time I realise I'm in the yard in my underpants, it's too late to retreat gracefully. The least I can do is shake the old man by the hand, but he avoids me, ignores me and sidles off, looking into the bottom of his empty glass. The kids wander off, and the two bikes watch over me from the flat ground. They aim at me and I walk away without a backward glance. I hear the roar of their engines, and rush back to the verandah. When I jump back into my bedroom, I can see them slither dead centre down the slope. They halt at the bit of verandah opposite my window, while I finish dressing. A third bike, which I had only just noticed, comes down from the volley-ball court with its engine switched off, and stops between the other two. I can't see their faces because of the helmets, but soon I notice the third rider is superior both in horsepower and in authority. His bike is much redder, as wide as a horse, with bronze spikes, mirrors, badges and regalia, as well as a spiral aerial all of four metres high. He's wearing rings on every finger and, in the glare of the morning sun, his fists look like two extra headlamps. He dismounts, and his two lieutenants do likewise. He comes on to the verandah still followed by the other two, and stops three steps from my window. In a voice that's even refined, he asks who I am and what I'm doing on that property. Several things pass through my mind, but I can't find a good reply. I look around thinking of the old man but the old man's not there. Ringsy asks me who I think I am and what the hell I'm doing on the property. I can see the kids lined up above the farm near the stream. I look at the ground, I'm barefooted, no time to get properly dressed. As if they were putting out cigars, his two shadows start rubbing their boots over the planks on the verandah, and so produce an unpleasant screech. The leader stuffs his hand in his leather jacket, he's going to take something out. He takes out an old-fashioned pocket watch, and says I've got five minutes to disappear from the map.

THREE

It was the old caretaker who gave me the crumpled notes to get back to the city. I ring my mother from the telephone in the bus station and hang up right away. In no way do I want to go to her house. All the same I want to drop in somewhere, I need to have a bath, I must wash my hair. I ring back, and Mummy must be sitting on her *chaise-longue*, leafing through a fashion magazine, fashions no longer for her, perhaps that's why she gets annoyed with the phone. I think it's only at the third ring that she gets up and drags herself over to the receiver, which is on a short flex in the passageway. Between the fifth and sixth ring she'll stop and cough, since old people can't cough on the move. Mummy gets hold of the phone only at the eighth ring, but some impulse makes me hang up a moment before. I give her time to get back to the *chaise-longue,* then ring again. This time I let it ring ten, twelve times, it could ring two hundred times for she's never going to answer me. And ever since my descent from the mountains some impulse has been telling me that today I'd end up ringing my ex-wife.

Her answering machine says she's at the Customs House, at such and such a number, and that you can leave a message after the tone. I ring the Customs House, a man answers in a gruff voice, I ask for her. She responds with "Hi," and I say "Hi, it's me," prepared to run the risk of hearing "Who's me?" but she lets out a "And what do you want?" that leaves no doubt she knows very well who I am. I only want a small favour and she says "I know." I need to talk to her now and she says "Not here."

The Customs House is an expensive boutique in a lively shopping mall in the most elegant quarter in the south of the city. It sells imported clothes, I think, I've never been inside. Now I go in for the first time, and don't make a good impression. A woman who had once been beautiful, and must be the owner, doesn't attend to me, but stands there eyeing me, looking my shoes over. The pale-faced shop assistant turns his face round, and my ex-wife behind the counter tightens her lips as if she is holding back a smile. I get closer to her, and see that she isn't, it's a pin she's holding between her lips, which she spits discreetly into the palm of her hand in order to say "Wait outside." I leave unruffled, running my finger over the clothes. These clothes are set out in the boutique quite untidily, not to give an impression of cheapness, but to make believe they aren't really on sale.

My ex-wife rushes past me, saying something about pizza on the mezzanine. I would prefer to eat outside, but she was always getting ahead of me, and is already walking her way up the escalator. She's wearing loose-fitting bermudas, but I can make out that same body of hers. She sits down on a bench in the café, and I get a glimpse of her breasts. She's bare-shouldered, and her skin is just the shade of someone who goes to the beach but doesn't sunbathe. If I told her everything I'm thinking now, she'd be delighted; but a moment later I almost ask her whether standing up all day in a boutique wouldn't give her varicose veins. Because we haven't spoken for six months, or because before that we'd said everything there was to say, or because over the last six months everything we said before turned into noise, it's hard to pick up the conversation.

She says "And what do you want?" in that same telephone voice. As she's got a menu, I don't know whether to choose a snack or to start telling her my problem. My ex-wife doesn't look at me or the menu; she's staring into space, as if she's on the phone. And she repeats "And what do you want?" overemphatically as if she's got a bad line. I tell her I'm in a tight corner, and she says "I know." I tell her there are people after me, and she says "Yes." I say they may kill me, and manage to stir her. But instead of apprehensive or panicky, she looks disgusted, as if dying was filthy. She says "You've sunk lower than I thought possible."

I ask for a mozzarella pizza, though I'm thinking the two of us are no longer suited to pizza, this snack bar, this shopping mall. I rather envy the heads sticking out in the void, coming up inquisitively one after another on the escalator, heads craning necks, sprouting bodies, sprouting feet that jump off on to the mezzanine, and turn into people who shake their heads, talk, blink, laugh and chew triangles of pizza up there.

My ex-wife finally clicks her tongue and says she's very sorry but she can't see how she can help me. The "I'm very sorry" comes with an accent from the heart, and her heart is pretty fickle. Now she's almost begging to help. Whatever I said to her, she would screw up her face but she'd do it. If I asked for money, she'd take her time but she'd give it. She could even take me back in the house till the danger's over. And I don't doubt she'd soon be talking like she used to, the same tone of voice in which she always said "I love you more than anything" when we met five years ago. She'd say 'I love you more than anything" in the middle of lunch, in the cinema, she'd say it in the supermarket, in front of other people; I thought it odd she said it all the time, but in the end I got used to it. Fickle heart. One day she came back from the doctor's, dragged me by the hand into the bedroom, she was very red-faced and said the results were positive, she was expecting a baby. I didn't understand. I didn't even know she'd

been to the doctor's. The news about having a son
rushed to my brain, flew around and couldn't shape
itself into an idea. I can't imagine what my reaction
could have been at the time, I don't remember if I
said anything. I can only remember that her face
went pale as I'd never seen it before, as if all her
blood had been sucked through a hole. She asked
me if I was a monster without feelings. But in time I
also got used to the idea of a son; better still a daughter, people say a daughter is closer to her father. I
even got to the point of naming the daughter after
my sister. Until late one afternoon my ex-wife came
back from the doctor's with a terrible face, she
slammed the bedroom door and said she'd put an
end to the child. In floods of tears she threw herself
on to the bed and kept asking "Are you happy now?
Are you happy now?" I think from that moment on
she stopped loving me more than anything.

My ex-wife checks her watch every twenty seconds, and I reckon she's worried about the owner of
the boutique. The waiter gives me the bill which she
hurries to pay, pulling notes from her wallet, and in
the rush she drops three credit cards. I go back with
her, and she starts to say goodbye on the escalator.
She walks off saying *"Ciao,"* typing the air with her

left hand, and I tell her to forget my old address, as I'm going to get a hotel room. She says "Good luck," but near the boutique I remember I've got some clothes in her house. She says there's not very much, that she's already stuffed it all into a suitcase, and that the boutique's errand-boy will take the case to my hotel. A lady with a bridge-playing face comes up, greets my ex-wife and asks about the tunic. She's about to go in the shop with the customer, but I tap her on the shoulder and tell her I can't book into a hotel without any luggage, with my clothes a mess and all unshaven, no porter's going to let anyone in looking like a down-and-out. She asks me to keep my voice down, but the owner of the Customs House is already at the door, with the pale shop assistant behind her, and the bridge player doesn't know whether she's coming or going. My ex-wife opens her bag, takes out a heart-shaped plastic key-ring and says "Go and get your case, then bring the keys back to me," managing to say these words practically without moving her lips.

I lived four and a half years with that woman. But I lived shut up with her, breakfast in bed, telephone

off the hook, not showing our faces in the street. An
ice-cream on the corner, at most an afternoon film,
shopping for dinner, and home. I started some jobs
she found for me, by the second week I fell ill, and
home again. In the last year she was the one who
began to go out to work. I argued she had a univer-
sity degree, she could expect better openings, and
said "You'll never adapt." But she did adapt, had a
real knack, really got into it, became sales manager
and never caught a single cold. I waited for her at
home. I got used to being at home without her, I
walked about naked, sang. I changed the lay-out of
the living room, planned to paper the walls. By now
I preferred home without my wife. Alone at home I
had more space to think about my wife, and I
thought most about her being away from home.
Sometimes she'd get back late at night, go in the
bathroom, meddle in the kitchen, switch on the television when there was no need, and that made me
kind of jealous about home. I'd rather not see her,
and often pretended to be asleep. In the morning, I
let her wake up alone, open and close drawers, turn
on the shower, switch on the blender and leave for
work. It was only then that my day began, walking
around at home, remembering my wife, sorting

things out. One day she suggested separating. I understood her and said that I'd go on thinking about her the same way all my life. But leaving home was more difficult. I wouldn't know how to remember home. It was inside home that I liked home, unthinkingly.

Here I am back with the keys in my hand, but I'm in no hurry; it's only her flat, an address, a ground-floor apartment on the side wing of an L-shaped building down a cul-de-sac in a damp part of town. It's a good way from here to there, and en route is my old neighbourhood, the streets I walked before I got married, chemists, bakeries, newspaper stalls, men and women I talked to, people I knew by name. The salty pizza has made my mouth dry. I stop in a bar and see there's no one there from my day. The barman's new as well and if I order a beer and don't hand over some cash it's quite likely he won't serve me. I ask for tap-water, but he doesn't hear me, stands there wiping the Formica counter with a wet cloth. At the end of the counter, a passage you can only walk along sideways leads to a lavatory with a heavy smell. There's also a wash-basin I lean over, but it's got no water. Past the lavatory, the corridor goes to an open storage space piled high with crates full of empty bottles. I feel like climbing over the crates. I climb up, reach the top and breathe in the clean air. The rear of the bar looks out on the rear of an apartment block. My hands manage to get a grip between the shards of glass cemented into the crest of the wall. If I bring my foot up level with the wall, it won't be difficult to hurl myself over the other side. I don't intend to jump to the other side. But neither can I see any sense in climbing down the crates, walking back past the stinking lavatory, past the barman and back into the street where I started, without even drinking a drop of water from the wash-basin.

I jump over the wall and fall into the playground belonging to the apartments. I walk quietly down some stairs into the underground car park; I don't think anyone saw me. A car has just driven out and the door to the street was left open. A group of youngsters are walking along the pavement towards me talking loudly, laughing and swinging keys around. I cross over the road and go into the tiny garden of a house where there is a ballet school. I walk round the house, recognise the backyard with its almond trees, and remember how an acquaintance of mine lived here, one that used to give parties and had a paralysed sister.

I can only remember one real friend. He was a few years older than me and said I had a future. He spent his time reading the newspapers, then specialist magazines, and afterwards told me they were all lies. He received letters from abroad, listened to the classics, was shortly going to publish a polemical treatise on some issue I've forgotten. He invented and wanted to teach me a language called Desperanto, and had organized the grammar and lots of vocabulary. He had one phase of devotion to edible sculpture; he built a whole marzipan city in his flat but never got to exhibit anything. He was also given to premonitions; he used to make such predictions that he'd take fright and go dumb for a week. And it appears that in his past he had a history that people of his generation knew and admired. He never talked to me about that history, which was why I admired him even more. In the bar, when he was drinking well over his limit, or when he got there already high, he'd recite poems. There were nights, generally Saturday nights when the bar was packed, he'd let his dark mop of hair fall over his forehead and insist on declaiming in French. I stood there ill at ease because he looked at me as he declaimed too loudly, and the other people at the table didn't understand the verse. He thought I did follow the drift. The

result was the two of us were left alone on that table
because the few people who can stand poetry can't
stand French.

I don't know what they thought of me, of my
friend, of our relationship. But when he was lucid,
saying things that came as revelations to me, the
others could hardly hear him, looked at him with a
dim expression. It was as if not only a table but
layers of time separated them from him. Sometimes
I thought he even preferred to say things that others
would only understand years later. The words he
searched for, his pauses, and above all his grave tone
of voice, made me believe he was one of those rare
people who can think and talk with time within
them. Today, however, as I try to remember what he
talked about, I only hear his voice, shorn of words.
And if I'm thinking about my friend it's because, as
I jump from the back of a state school to the grounds
of a house in course of demolition, I realise he lives
or lived here in this treeless avenue, in the oldest
building in the area, a grey building set back from
the road and next to a bar.

I intend to walk on. It's 3 p.m., and quite likely
my friend's still asleep. I haven't got anything to tell
him, and he'll be in no mood to open his mouth

either. If I go up, neither do I know if he'll open the door; he'll see me through the spy-hole, and perhaps he'll act dead till I clear off. If he does open the door, perhaps I'll be surprised to find him the same as he was five years ago. Perhaps he'll seem only a bit shorter than he was, a couple of centimetres at the most, but he'll probably be wearing the same shirt outside his trousers, with the same coffee stain on the collar. He won't have lost a single hair from the black mop that falls down over his forehead exactly the way it did last time I saw him. I would almost want to hug him, go into his flat like in the old days, stretch out on his living-room sofa and sleep till morning. But when I take a closer look at him, perhaps his stature will bemuse me; my friend was taller, only slightly, but he was. Five years later, nothing odd in his being round-shouldered, having a distended stomach and a slightly twisted spine. But he'll stand up straight, as if they'd only sawn two centimetres off his shins. That won't seem sincere. I won't know how to cope with someone who gives the impression of being a copy of my friend. Who will run his hand through his hair the same way, which I'll find enervating, since the more perfect the copy the greater the sense of being cheated. And he'll bite the right side of his tongue, the way he did when he didn't like something, because perhaps he'll suspect I'm a copy too. And he'll see me standing there, know I've a bitter taste in my mouth, and won't offer me a glass of water. And he'll say "Excuse me" imitating a baritone voice, and slam the door in my face.

I can see turmoil in front of my friend's block. A crowd, a police van, two patrol cars, a vehicle from the morgue, several press cars, police diverting the traffic. In the midst of the throng, I realise a crime's been committed, someone's been stabbed and strangled to death. A second police van's siren whirs towards us, and the hurly-burly carries me to the centre of the incident. A piece of red string separates out the pavement in front of the old building into a kind of boxing ring. The television people are interviewing the concierge under the awning over the lobby. It must be a pain to film, because the concierge keeps looking at the ground and mumbling, looks like a convict. I think he's the criminal, but soon realise he's just very embarrassed about the building. The reporter asks if the victim was in the habit of inviting boys in, and the concierge nods more in confession than in agreement. The interview is hampered by a shortish, Indian-faced woman in a headscarf, who disentangles herself from a policeman and attacks the concierge, shouting out "Say you know my son, you miserable so-and-so!" The policeman picks up the squat Indian woman and puts her outside the cordoned-off area. She ducks back under the string and addresses the onlookers. She asks "The television's here, isn't it?" and "Won't somebody interview me?" A youth who introduces himself as a reporter on the *Diario Vigilante* asks what the suspect was doing at the scene of the crime. She says "What suspect you mean?" and "What scene of the crime?" and says "My son was coming to see me, was arrested entering the building, if he was a suspect, he'd have run for it," and then says "Who ever heard of a suspect running off inside?" Without more ado I start rooting for the Indian mother. The *Diario Vigilante* reporter wants to ask something else, but she interrupts him to say she's been working at number 204 for fifteen years, that everyone knows who she is, that the misery over there knows her son and won't defend him because he's colour-prejudiced. She goes to attack the concierge again but is held back by the policeman. Another TV reporter asks the concierge whether the

victim was a homosexual. The concierge mutters "I
don't know, I've never seen such a thing." The Indian tells Radio Primazia they arrested her son because he wasn't carrying his papers. She says "My
son was coming back from the beach, it's not a crime
to go to the beach, no one goes to the beach with
their papers in their trunks." A fellow behind me
says he's from the newspapers as well and asks
"Was the queer an arty type or what?" She answers
"I don't know about the queer, seems he was a gym
teacher." The reporter from TV Promontorio comes
up and says "Let's hear from the mother of the main
suspect." At this the Indian woman goes out of her
mind, grabs the reporter by the lapels, bursts into
tears and bellows into the microphone "He isn't a
criminal! My son's a decent lad!" but the camera-
man who's climbed on to the bonnet of the truck
shouts down "It's no good, nothing's recorded,
change the battery!" The Indian stops crying, looks
at the press and asks "How could that son of mine
who may be sick strangle a gym teacher?" The reporter from TV Promontorio comes back to ask her
to repeat what she said before, he thought it was
strong stuff. I was really wanting her not to repeat
it, but it's too late now, she's crying more than ever

and bellowing "He isn't a criminal! My son's a decent lad! He's an honest, hardworking boy!" I would rather she didn't act out such a scene because it sounds messy, and it's going to compromise her son even more on television. And just when she said her son was honest and hardworking, the youth appeared in the lobby, and the camera caught him walking along the pavement, wearing rubber briefs in a jaguar-skin pattern. He's black, the size of four mothers, in fact more flab than muscle. The police push him along, handcuffed, his body bent forward, but he looks up and laughs. He laughs for the camera on the bonnet, laughs at the neighbours' windows, laughs for nobody, laughs at the sun, and I think it's not exactly laughter on his lips. His mother tries to grab him, one girl shouts out "Hey, horny!" another "You junkie!" and he's thrown into the back of the van. The mother yells and runs her fingernails across the rear door of the van, trying to get in through the cracks. She finally manages to get arrested and locked up in the second van. The two vehicles drive off, their sirens wailing to a chorus of jeers.

Now two porters in the uniform of the Coroner's Court emerge from the building with the body

wrapped in sheets and blankets, and all the onlookers, even the people in the bar, go quiet. I can even
sense the silence flowing, and it's like a silence coming from under the ground, and the ground unrolling
like a carpet smothering every sound as far as the
other side of the avenue. The body passes right before my eyes. The first porter, swollen-nosed, is
holding it under the armpits, letting the head hang
down like a bag. The second one is holding it behind
the knees and walks unsteadily, squeezing and ex-
tending the body like a pair of bellows. The dead
man's feet are still bare, and are well cared for, only
the soles are rather grimy, but the feet look enormous to me, feet which must take a size twelve or
twelve and a half. They fit the body into a compartment in the morgue vehicle. I expected blood would
drip, but it didn't.

The departure of the morgue wagon unleashes the
traffic. The television crews leave, the demarcation
string is removed, people circulate, and the concierge seems to feel the sudden loss of glory, even
though he'd been a timid performer; he looks up,
then right round before retiring inside the block. Just
one police patrol car is left with two wheels on the
pavement and two policemen in the entrance. If I

tried to go in now to visit my friend, they'd certainly question me. I go into the bar next door, and the counter is cramful of elbows. There's a lavatory at the back but the sink has been ripped off the wall.

On the way to my ex-wife's house, my thirst was supplemented by a frantic need to urinate. The reservoir I'd imagined I'd drunk is nearly bursting my bladder, as I struggle in vain with the key to the door that was once mine. The lock gives me a hard time, it must have been changed, and now it opens to the right, and there are three turns in the lock, and I can't stand it any more, I'm only a few metres from my target, the urine's been alerted and it's already on course. I run across the living room, unzipping my fly, into a bathroom and it isn't that, it's the kitchen, but at this stage no way can I hold back the thick piss spurting over the marble top, and into the stainless-steel sink full of yesterday's dishes and glasses lined with dregs of red wine. Nausea follows the painful relief. I open the icebox after water and am met by the sweet smell of guava. I walk back to the living room feeling dizzy, and have the impression it's been turned round. They must have blocked

off two windows and opened another two on the wall
opposite.

The taps also want to turn the other way, a caprice
I'm constrained to give way to, feeling utterly ham-
handed. The shower water falls on my skin and
doesn't run down but ricochets. Patiently I manage
to control the temper of the water, and my shower
and I begin to recognise each other. Its oddities and
those of my body start to come together again. I pull
the shower curtain to, and am consumed by the
steam. I gradually lose sight of my body and everything else. One day, in the sauna, my friend said the
ancients called them laconic baths. Maybe. I can't
see the connection myself. I only know it'll take me
years to hit upon a shower to rival this. It won't be
at all easy. The shower in my flat had a jet that was
well rounded, correct, even, solid, it was an idiot
shower. Not here, here I'm fulfilled. Besides, perhaps the ancients weren't as slow as they appear,
and they didn't like lengthy bathtime meditations.
Laconic baths. I for one was going to spend the rest
of my days in the steam. But I'd better have a break,
my feet are quite limp, and heavy. I can feel the
water up to my shins. I try to look, and the tray
seems bottomless. I switch the shower off, let the

steam clear, and see the pool of black water on the floor of the tray. It's all clogged up. I can see brown water on the bathroom tiles, a dirty-yellow invasion of the living room. Gingerly I get out of the shower. There are two towels on the bathroom hanger. She must keep the others in her bedroom wardrobe. I reckon that with five or six towels I can build a dam in the living room and prevent disaster. I open the wardrobe and in the inside mirror spot my muddy footprints over her pearl-grey carpet. She'll think I did it on purpose. Anyway I've got to clear out. I can't stand still here. My case must be at the back of the wardrobe. To get hold of my case, I have to take her clothes out of the wardrobe. I see a tweed coat that looks like a man's but it's not mine. Now the clothes are spread all over the room, just like the boutique. She can only think I did it on purpose. But the case isn't at the back of the wardrobe. I'm not getting anywhere standing here. I must find that case. I sit down on the bed that was once ours. She didn't say where she'd put the case.

FOUR

I'm not getting anywhere standing here. I can't hide for ever from a man I don't know. I need to find out if he intends to keep pursuing me. When this fellow gets tired of ringing my bell and leaves, I'll up and after him. It'll be dusk, he'll close the case for the day, and decide to walk home. He'll be tired, he'll be getting hunchbacked and will deplore the wasted day. I expect he lives in a terraced house not far from here, even so, it's morning before he gets back.

Through the window I'll see him no sooner arrive
than be saying goodbye to his pregnant wife. The
pregnant wife will never know whether he's going to
kiss her, or whether he's getting more hunchbacked
by the day. He'll leave home and cross the road without seeing me. Will walk into the firm, a building on
fifty-five floors, where his department operates on
the third-level basement. I'll be kept out through
lack of identification but can spy on him on the
closed-circuit television. He'll spend the morning
checking his index cards against the documentation
from the central archive that will be on the floor.
He'll be behind on lots of jobs, not to mention the
work he does elsewhere to make up his salary. He'll
receive instructions to track down an Arab who lives
in the suburbs, and whom he's already pursued on
other occasions, unsuccessfully. The firm's drivers
won't take on suburban jobs, and the taxi allowance
will be withdrawn. He'll leave the building quite reluctant to take three buses and a train to track down
an Arab who's never at home. He won't notice that I
follow him into the cinema on the corner, where
they're showing a porno film. I'll get myself a seat in
the row behind him, and I'll get to know the nape of
my persecutor's neck. He'll walk out on the film in

the scene with the two pregnant women, and stroll crestfallen through the city thinking about the Arab. It'll be nightfall when he recognises the mosaic on the pavement outside the L-shaped building where I'll be living with my ex-wife. Then he'll remember to chase after me, make it home in time for dinner, and before bed draw up a phoney report. He won't suspect I can see him outside my door, straightening up in front of the spy-hole, and that thick, bell-pressing thumb has a filthy nail. By the time he's hammering on the door, I'll be in bed. He'll try to break the door down, but I'll be sound asleep. I'll be dreaming he's shouting out my name, and it's like a woman who's gone hoarse. It's her.

I jump out of bed. My ex-wife bounces into the house, but only manages to say "You . . ." She wasn't expecting to see me naked when I open the door, and baulks at the panorama in her flat. She sweeps round the living room, stops in front of the bathroom door, walks backwards, walks as if she's drunk, goes into her bedroom and collapses weeping on to her bed. I thought she was going to say "You happy now?" but she doesn't say another word, stays face down, sobs with her entire body, and I don't know what to do. I can only see her body struggling, down her left rather than her right side, and the sight suddenly arouses my desire for her. Not even I understand this desire, it goes against me. It has no sense, because if she called me, and said through moist lips "Come here," or "I'm yours," or "Do whatever you want to me," I'd probably feel no desire at all. But she's crying from head to toe, her feet twist inwards, her hands pull her hair out, in a fit that amazes me, an amazement that increases my desire. I have no wish to desire a woman torn in this way. And if she sees me in this state, she'll think it's on purpose. I try thinking about other things, and remember she always kept our suitcases under the bed. Mine is quite old and imitation leather. I put some jeans on and a white T-shirt with no advertising slogan, and also at the bottom of the case I find some nearly new sneakers that fit me though I don't know if they're mine.

It's dark and the heat's stifling. The suitcase is not so heavy, but it's uncomfortable to carry, it attracts attention. I stop on the kerb and pretend I'm waiting for a taxi. A taxi brakes and I walk on with my case, pretending to examine the numbers on the buildings. I turn the corner down a road without much movement; perhaps a mugger will relieve me of my suitcase. After my daytime snooze and wash, I could walk around till morning, and no commitments. But a man without commitments carrying a suitcase is wedded to the fate of his suitcase. It forces me to walk along all lopsided in a hurry. When I come to, I'm at the foot of the hills leading to my sister's house. I guess this was the tortuous path I'd make if I were blind. And these are the steep slopes I climb like water flowing down.

It's some time since I was here at night, and, when I saw the new condominium lights in the distance, I thought it was a film set. An array of searchlights turns the pavement slabs blue, slices under the branches of the trees, and dazzles all visitors. I can't make out the guard who asks me to identify myself. There's more than one guard, there are several voices repeating my name like an echo round the sentry-box. They mass-produce replies as well, and I have to listen to "Not on the list," "Not on the list," "Not on the list." Then a loud laugh comes and goes, and a cicada gets caught up in my hair. I don't know what list they're talking about, I just want to leave a case at number 16, and there must be a prob-

lem because the voices start to change. They ask
what I've got in that suitcase, and before I can reply,
a silhouette wrenches the handle from me. Despite
the jolt, I'm pleased; the case has met its fate and
I'm free of it at last. I think how I'm free of everything, how the city awaits me, but when I attempt to
retreat, somebody sinks their claws into my arm and
drags me into the spotlight. A guy in a beige, double-
breasted coat gives me a hug, then runs his hands
down my back, pats my buttocks, groin, thighs, behind my knees, and is checking out my ankles when
a big black car with smoked-glass windows draws
up. The front window opens a fraction and the man
at the driving-wheel says a long woman's name. The
sentry-box thinks it's all right and activates the electronic gate, but the car doesn't move off. A woman's
voice asks whether I want to get in. I look for the
woman beyond the glare from the sentry-box, but the
voice comes from the shadowy depths of the black
car. All the guards leave the sentry-box to attend to
the voice, say "No problem, madam," and then the
chauffeur gets out and opens the back door for me.

She's my sister's skinny friend whom I've been on
"hello" terms with for years. She's holding opera
glasses to her lips, asks me if I like it straight and

offers me a swig from the opera glasses. Then she grabs a bottle of whisky from behind the seat, saying you can't trust my brother-in-law, let alone the whisky he gives out. She tries to decant the whisky into the neck of the opera glasses, but the car skids on the slope, she bursts out laughing as the whisky soaks the short skirt of her suit. She says "Oh, fuck." There's a traffic jam at the top of the slope, and she decides to jump out right there. She wiggles her way on her stilettos over the cobbles. She walks into the party with her shoes in her hand and the opera glasses round her neck.

If I'd known my sister was throwing a party, at least I'd have shaved. I'd have chosen suitable clothes, though I can see all types there: the banker type, the playboy type, ambassadors, singers, adolescents, architects, landscape designers, psychoanalysts, dancers, actresses, military men, foreigners, columnists, judges, philanthropists, ministers, gamblers, builders, economists, fashion designers, smugglers, advertising men, drug addicts, landowners, men of letters, astrologers, photographers, filmmakers, politicians, and my name wasn't on the list. Some of these guests are sitting at round tables arranged in the garden. As I don't know anyone, I feel free to walk round the tables and pick up fragments of speeches, arguments, and laughter. Other people are standing on the expanse of lawn in a series of circles. I can see how each circle behaves, how it closes, how it opens, how one circle incorporates others. I can see some circumferences that are over-distended, until they burst like bubbles, setting off new circles of conversation. I see sleepy circles that remain circles because of geometry, rather than content. I try to accompany issues that leave one circle to animate another and another and another like gear wheels. At times the whole party seems to take a breather, and you can hear a chord from the orchestra that's playing dance tunes indoors.

I walk down a torchlit path where there are no more circles; people are talking in pairs, in muffled tones. A young man walks by carrying a glass of white wine in each hand. The young man's got a pretty face, a bit too pretty, and disappears into a hollow away from the torches. The sky's the same raw sky as last night, and I still haven't seen my sister. The translucent circle of the swimming pool emerges from the gloom like an anti-well. I skirt round the swimming pool, the changing rooms, the tennis court, and sense the branches starting to wave in that hollow. I try to reach the end of the property, by the edge of the woods, but the wind blows sand into my eyes. I think it unlikely my sister's there, and almost knock over the very pretty young man who's walking back up all uncombed. He walks by looking over my head, still carrying two full glasses of white wine, then turns down a short-cut unfamiliar to me. The path ends on a level beneath the house, where a steep bank of earth is compacted between the supports, not a place anyone would arrange a rendezvous. Bolted on to the joints of the steel and concrete pillars which support the pyramid are yellow light reflectors that attract and decimate the insects. The young man wanders fitfully around under the concrete floor of the main lounge, which is swaying to the rhythm of the orchestra. He walks with his stomach held in, attempting to balance the glasses, and keeps an earnest face, like a photographic model. He stops in front of a light reflector and suddenly twists his head towards me, pushes back the hair falling over his face, and asks "What's the time?" but I'm in a T-shirt and it's obvious I've not got a watch.

I walk up the stone steps back into the garden, where there is a fresh bevy of guests. I make my way

towards the house, and in the hallway get mixed up
with a group of girls who are leaving the dance fan-
ning themselves, blowing down inside the necklines
of their black blouses. Two men, in their fifties,
come in from the garden: tanned, drinking vodka,
both in white shoes, with faces like members of the
Yacht Club. The taller one is sporting a navy-blue
blazer with gold buttons, and uses brilliantine on his
greying hair. Shorty with the dripping armpits is
wearing a corset under his clothes, which deforms
the belly it's supposed to disguise; that's my sister's
husband, and he's pointing at me. I slip through the
girls in black, into the house, look for a bathroom,
but I'm intercepted by a boy who reckons he knows
me. He shakes me by the shoulders and says "You
were right! You got it!" He says other things I don't
understand, very quickly and emphatically, as if he's
giving me a horse-race commentary. My brother-in-
law catches up with me, Greyhair in tow, and introduces me with the words "This is him." Greyhair
says it's always the same, every self-respecting family has its drop-out. My brother-in-law tries to defend
me by saying I'm something of an artist, slapping me
on the vertebrae with a "That's right, isn't it?" He
says his friend has a house in the country next to our

farm, but has stopped spending the summer there because the area's gone downhill. He says his friend says I let our farm turn into a doss-house. I see an anxious waiter walk by, I slip off in search of a whisky and penetrate the lounge where people are dancing and clapping in time with the music. I walk around the lounge behind the orchestra, and finish up in the dining room. I approach the buffet, hovering between canapés and prawns impaled on a cabbage, when I catch "doss-house full of tramps and delinquents." My brother-in-law says "Can't credit it," tugs at my T-shirt and asks "Did you know?" Greyhair: "See for yourself." Brother-in-law: "I've never been, my wife detests the place." Greyhair: "It was a paradise." Brother-in-law: "What about the police?" Greyhair: "I got fed up with complaining." I don't know what else they said, because I'm watching the wind rise up, blow out one torch after another along the garden paths, and now knock over the garden furniture. Waiters gallop over the lawn with coloured tablecloths, looking as if they're celebrating some championship.

I open a door into the pantry, and the whirl of trays diverts me into another room, which looks misshapen, deserted and white, which I suspect may be

a room for hunting trophies without trophies. My
brother-in-law's voice seems to echo round the high
walls: "My wife detests the place," "My wife detests
the place." I catch sight of the winter garden, the
inside patio in darkness, the oval table, the big staircase, and there's no one there either. It's an attrac-
tive staircase, wide rather than high, down which a
couple could come dancing. If I went up to the second floor now, nobody would see me as nobody saw
me the first time.

It was a Sunday at the beginning of this summer
when I paid my sister a surprise visit. She was in the
pool with some friends, and I remember she was in
a wine-coloured swimsuit. I had a dip, rubbed cream
on my skin, sunbathed, but didn't fit in because they
only talked about their travels, about interesting
people and cities I'd never seen. I wandered around
the gardens unnoticed, went into the house and had
a beer in the kitchen, where a lad dangling from
scaffolding was cleaning the grime off the windows.
My brother-in-law had gone out, I think their daughter had too, and most of the servants were on their
day off. I turned on the sound system, walked in my
sandals through the living rooms, and came to this
staircase. I saw myself climbing the big staircase. I

saw myself not really wanting to go, but almost being called from my sister's bedroom. I don't know why but I got the feeling my sister wanted me to look at her room, and had cleared family, friends and servants out of the way. I walked along a corridor full of fake doors, knowing full well which was her bedroom. I didn't need to go in to know what it was like, for I already imagined I knew it intimately. But curiosity is indeed made of what we already know through our imagination. I went into her room which was still untidy and recognised spaces, temperature, luminosity, pastel shade, oriental engravings on the wall. In the middle of all that, the couple's bed seemed an absurd installation; I could never imagine my sister and her husband sleeping in the same room.

Today I find the door ajar, the room in darkness, and I rather regret I walked in. The orchestra's brass section hits me at full blast, but I'm certain I heard a sigh, a sigh of a voice I know. I feel once I'm used to the half-dark I'll see two bodies in bed. The man may be the pretty one with the wine glasses, his shoulders will be very white. And the woman'll see I'm there, but won't manage to break off, won't want to break off, and her chestnut-brown hair will be

spread out like a fan on the sheet, and she'll look at
me as she's never looked at me before. I'll try to turn
my back on her, but I'm stuck there. I'll intend to
say "That's enough," but other words will pop out.
I'll determine not to see anything, which will be in-
genuous; I'll close my eyes with such an impetus that
my eyelids will fall to the ground.

My vision clears and there's nobody in the room.
There's the impeccable bed, with an antique-lace
counterpane and bolsters. That Sunday the bed disgusted me, with the husband's side all rucked up,
and I had seen enough. I was just leaving when I
heard steps in the corridor. If I'd asked my sister, of
course she would have left her friends by the pool
and been delighted to show me the whole house. But
if she were to find me in her bedroom, catch me
wearing wet trunks in her bedroom, it would be la-
mentable. I rushed through a door by the bed, and
got into a closet that was in fact another room, with
a view over the inside patio, as clear as an aquarium
and with no other way out. Footsteps came into the
bedroom, and I was trapped. I thought she'd come
into the closet to change her swimsuit because
there's a time when they think they have to change.
And I'd hide among her winter clothes, and in the

mirror I'd see her about to shed her wine-coloured swimsuit. And she might spin round and surprise me from the same angle, or perhaps she'd just sense my presence and want to strip off casually for me. But the steps zigzagging across the room weren't hers. They were chambermaid sounds, curtains being drawn and windows tipped open, the glasses, ash-trays, newspapers and supplements spread around being collected up. I realised it was going to be a lengthy cleaning session, for it wasn't just a quick Sunday whip-round, pulling the sheets out and stuff-ing them back under the mattress; these were the generous, flag-sheet flaps of a chambermaid in a grand hotel.

Today I'm entering the closet for the second time, and, even without the light on, I know where I'm going. I'm on her side and brush against night-dresses, veils, dresses, send silk sleeves swaying. I know half of the left wall is taken up by shoes which dazzled me that Sunday: boots, moccasins, pumps, a lot of models in every colour. Behind the shoe com-partment there's a recess I remember well, because I squeezed in there when the maid came in the closet, spent a long time arranging the coathangers and finished the work. In my corner there was a shelf full of boxes which I started opening and found more shoes, still virgin. Then I opened a round kind of hat box, and inside there was another round box, then another and another, like Russian dolls. In the last little hat box I found a light-colored chamois bag. I put my hand inside and touched my sister's jewels.

Whether on display or on a woman's body, my eyes may not discern the illustrious jewel. But there was a kind of breathing from those stones, and my hand quickly caught their nature. My hand grew stiff inside the bag and was unable to let go of the stones. I did though, retied the chamois string round the top of the bag, and put the bag with the jewels back inside the box in the box in the box in the box. I remembered the conversation by the swimming pool, the women saying how nobody in the city was crazy enough to go round wearing jewels. "In Europe it's meganormal," one was saying, "it's even meganormal to wear jewels on the subway." That meant, for her next trip, my sister would come to get her jewels from that chamois bag. If anything was missing, however trifling, the maid would be out on the street. I left the closet thinking I was a fine fellow. I said goodbye from a distance to the people by the pool, but I don't think even my sister heard me.

Now I grope around the shelf with the boxes and pick out the hat box. I lift up successive lids and smooth down the chamois. Dividing the jewels up among the four pockets of my jeans is a gesture swift like a reflex. An act so silent and obscure that not even I witness it. An unthinking act, and an act so manual it can be forgotten. That can be denied, an act that may not have been.

As I leave the closet for the bedroom, a woman's "Hello" freezes me to the spot. This time there really is someone in the bed. She comes barefoot towards me, and it's my sister's skinny friend holding some lipstick. I think she's going to put some on her lips, instead she lifts the lipstick to her nostril and breathes in deeply. She says "Oh fuck," and throws it away. She pulls her body towards mine and says "It's gone sticky." She kisses me, presses her thighs against mine, and must feel the jewels sticking out through my pockets. I disentangle myself, try to leave, but she shouts out "Look at this!" She undoes two jacket buttons, slowly baring her left breast, and says "You don't know me." In the corridor, I can still hear "I'm really sweet!" and "I'm megacrazy!"

The stairs are clear, the winter garden, the trophy room, and with one leap I reach the spiral stairs that should lead to the garage; that should lead into the garage, if the door weren't locked and the key missing. I have to go via the pantry. There I find myself among men who seem from another circumstance, each carrying their parcel or supermarket bag, each looking as if they didn't enjoy the party. Unthinkingly, I join this retinue of sadly garbed men leaving by the service door. In the morning light, bristles beginning to dot their faces, they're like discarded men, carrying their parcelled waiters under their arms. I'm also handed an envelope by a young lad who says "A tip from the master of the house." I sit down with them in one of the minibuses waiting outside. We depart in silence. The minibus drives aimlessly around the city, and nobody speaks up. Occasionally someone gets off as if he's seasick. After lots of coming and going, there's just me and the driver. We park in a square, and I'm not sure if it's the end of the line or if the petrol's run out. I open the door and walk towards the bus station.

FIVE

The bus is an old crate that climbs up the mountain jam-packed. Some passengers are standing, I've lost my place by the window, the person next to me is corpulent and I've got jewels in my pockets, I'm sitting on stones, but it feels comfortable. I think it's the rain. Shiny tarmac, deep green trees like screwed-up clothing, this is my road. On a sharp right bend, I feel my neighbour's shoulder pressing into mine, and laugh to myself. I laugh because I remember when we used to drive out to the farm with my parents, I and my sister in the back seat. A bend on my side, and I'd throw myself on top of her, going "Whooooooo." A bend on her side, and she'd fall on me: "Whoooooooo." That reminiscence strikes me so forcefully that I can even smell my sister's head, a smell she said was her hair and I said was her head, because she changed shampoo and the smell stayed the same, and she would say I was just a kid and got everything wrong, but I was sure it was her head that smelled, then she asked me what the smell was like, and I got embarrassed because I wouldn't know how to explain a smell, and she'd say "That's got you," but the fact is I never forgot, I've smelled the heads of lots of women and I've never felt anything similar. Now the bend twists to the left, and unintentionally I let my body fall against my neighbour's, almost going "Whooooooo." Perhaps he's also got nice memories, perhaps he had a sister like mine, a head smelling like hers, and will also be laughing to himself. Indeed I think he likes it, because it's an S-bend and now he's toppling over on to me.

It can't really have rained so much in my child-hood. But there I am as a boy, and it's raining. Now my sister's adolescent, and it's raining. We're both in the stream, in our swimsuits, sunburnt, and it's raining. The sun, there's the sun on the cement wall, I can see the cat stretched out on the cement in the sun, and it's raining. Maybe it wasn't raining then; the rain imprinted itself later on my memory. And I'd already forgotten the jokes, when the hefty fellow by the window rolls his whole body over my side, on a bend that is much longer than it used to be. I'm not into that any more, and start to think it's a nuisance. Two hundred metres further on, he's back again. I'll complain, poke him in the arm, but when I look at the fellow's hands, the fellow's got hands of wax. I swear his hands are made of wax, I'd never seen hands that colour, except my father's crossed hands in his coffin. I look him in the face, and it's made of the same wax, the same olive-grey lack of colour, and has the expression of someone who's going nowhere any more. Perhaps I should shout out, get well away, tell them to stop the bus, but nobody's upset to see a dead man next to me. The people standing opposite my seat think everything's normal. Except a fat, pop-eyed black woman, but she's looking at me, not the corpse. Perhaps I should really do something, but I'm almost at my stop. I get up carefully, prop up the dead man so he doesn't fall over, and the fat black woman immediately takes my place. I say "Brialuz service station" to the driver, and look at the back of the bus. When it brakes, I get the impression the dead man leans forward, knocks his forehead on the seat in front, then slumps backwards. I jump off the bus, take four steps over the verge, swing my body round, and see the dead man's face staring at me from the centre of the window. The bus delays its departure, and I can't escape the dead man. I walk up and down on the grass, and, whichever way I go, the dead man's looking straight at me, without even turning his head round. Looking like a mute television newscaster. The bus drives slowly off, and now the dead man's head swings back round, still looking at me, as if his neck were a screw.

The gate to the farm is neither open nor shut. Set free after five years in the mud, it lashes to and fro like a sail in a storm. To bring it under control, I have to wait till it snaps towards me, dodge round like a boxer and immobilise it with my haunch. I'm concluding this manoeuvre when a brand-new van turns up, painted a metallic orange and with no number-plate. The van goes into a fast skid, spits mud everywhere, but keeps its spotless gleam, the colour of the sun. The driver's careful and brakes three metres from the entrance, so sparing me a mud-bath. I signal him to go through first, as it's no trouble to hold the gate in that position. But a lanky mulatto, in dark glasses, his hair brushed flat, an earring in his left ear, gets out of the rear door and invites me to get in. I sit between him and someone who looks like his twin brother, ring, hair, the whole bit, behind is the red-haired, ring-laden driver and his co-pilot, older than the others, broken-nosed and almost bald. The gate, which is in the meantime kept open and tremulous, buffets the air as soon as we're through.

We go down the track as far as the stream, then turn off to the old guest-house. The whitewashed construction with a blue timber frame now seems only a base for the sizeable asbestos roof covering an adjacent pavilion where a kind of repair shop has been set up. Our van parks in between a burnt-out carcass and a jeep painted with primer; along-side are some chassis and open engines, the three motor bikes I've already encountered, plus two pick-up trucks, a repro antique sports car, and a convertible with a foreign number-plate. Behind the garage are half a dozen trailers lined up in convoy. The twin walks me to the last, makes me get in, then locks the door from the outside.

It would be a spacious trailer if the stacks of steel drums and crates left any space. Oxygen is in short supply and the place smells of acetone. I sit down on a small patch of floor, opposite the only unblocked window. It suddenly goes dark, and I take a few seconds to realise a dappled cow is leaning its head against the glass. The cow's head fits exactly into the window, and settles down there. She's a tired cow. From time to time her eyelid licks her eye, in a grave movement I soon learn to predict. I also get used to the saliva from the corner of her mouth that hangs down some four inches and goes up, hangs down and goes up again. Occasionally the dappled cow swings her jaw forward lightly, as if asking "What's up?" or "What's the matter?" or "What do you think about it?" When the twin appears at the door, I reckon a long time has gone by. But it wasn't time that weighed heavily, perhaps because I was waiting in cow time.

The twin switches the light on and positions himself opposite me, blotting out both window and cow. He's got thin, very long legs and is wearing leather trousers which squeeze and spread out his balls. His belt is a bronze chain. His hands are on his hips and his padded jacket is half-opened, revealing the tip of a barrel sticking out of a holster. He's still in his Ray-Bans and seems excited, because he starts to rub the sole of his boot over the floor of the trailer. We are separated by a low crate, where I set out the jewels: a diamond plaque, a gold watch, a four-stringed pearl necklace with diamond clasp, a ruby-and-diamond pendant, a sapphire brooch, a pair of sapphire earrings, a set of emerald earrings, ring, and bracelet, a platinum ring with aquamarine, a diamond engagement ring, a solitaire.

He pushes his glasses up and stands there silent in front of the jewels, but doesn't touch them. Then he purses his lips up the size of a fig, says "Mmm, mmm," nods approvingly and says "Good stuff." He leaves with a bang of the door and is soon back, but it must be the other twin because he comes in and starts breaking up my exhibition.

He sweeps the jewellery like biscuits off the crate with the back of his hand and says "We don't get mixed up with this crap." As I go to pick up the

stones, something hits me violently in the right
cheek—his knee or boot toe-cap or karate chop—
and the shock is worse than the initial pain. The
centre of pain fades and irradiates to the rest of my
head and surrounds it, and it's outside my head that
the pain hurts. Enclosed by pain, I myself can't feel
anything, I've gone blind and deaf.

Still blinded, I begin to hear a quarrel I don't understand, but I know it's the twins; they're arguing
in voices that are so similar they seem like voices of
one man contradicting himself. Afterwards one
leaves, and the other picks me up by the scruff of
the neck and takes me out. When I recover my sight,
I'm on my way into another trailer, bigger than the
first one, smelling new, with wall-to-wall carpeting
that's soft underfoot. The redhead is bent over a
purple, glass-topped table fingering my jewels. On
the table there's also a crystal glass, a dagger with a
carved ivory handle, a portable television, medicine
bottles and tubes, a porcelain Buddha, a mother-of-
pearl case and a telephone shaped like a tortoise.
The twins stand by the door like two columns. And
the fourth man, with wispy hair and a boxer's nose,
lies back in an armchair, legs spread wide, observing
me. Finally the redhead clears his throat to indicate

he's going to speak and does talk while he looks at
the jewels, in a voice that's unexpectedly gentle, if
not feminine. He says "The merchandise is good."
He picks up the brooch, closes his left eye, turns the
sapphire against the light from the window and says
"It's fine." He puts the jewels away in the eight
pockets of his velvet jacket and tells me indirectly
"We're in business," while looking at the ex-boxer.
When I try to leave, one twin blocks my way; one
offers me water, that turns into blood in my mouth.

It's still daylight, the sun's almost shining, and I
wonder if it ever got to rain inside the farm. The
track and vegetation are dry as far as the gate, and
beyond that nothing is visible; the farm is an island
bobbing in the void, a thick mist obliterating its out-
line. If I walked through the gate now, I don't think
I'd find anywhere to take my foot. I walk down the
dirt track, and notice how it forks off just before the
stream. They've cut a rough trail through a bamboo
thicket leading to a new glade where they've set up
a camp-site. There are dozens of camouflage-green
polyester tents I couldn't see the other night because
I went in blindly, and missed the following morning
because I left in a hurry. I wander through little tents
of different shapes: prisms, pyramids, marquees, ig-

loos, snails, and not a sign of life. Near the plank
bridge I hear an electronic noise, the sound of a
football match coming from a caterpillarish tent. I
want to ask the score, like anyone does, even though
I don't know who's playing. Kneeling in front of the
flap, I push the mosquito net aside, and someone
protests with a raucous moan.

I head towards the main house, and think I
glimpse shadows crawling down the hillsides towards the flanks of the camp-site like an army in
tatters. I double my pace, go in the house via the
kitchen, and find the girl with the head of hair in
front of the charcoal stove. Perched on her stool, she
holds the enormous wooden spoon with both hands,
rowing in rather than stirring the soup in the pot.
She stops for a moment when she sees me, then
smiles and steps up her hip-swaying. The old caretaker is sleeping stiffly in a diagonal across the side
of a chair, a red nylon windcheater hiding his head,
and a plastic hood round hair that has just been dyed
mahogany. The din of a gang of twenty kids attack-
ing the house will wake him up. They bring damp
notes that the old man collects up from one hand
after another and throws into the rucksack. It's only
then he sees me and looks embarrassed and gets

emotional with a "God bless you, God bless you," and insists on accompanying me to my old bedroom.

The girl with the head of hair soon starts knocking. I'm already stretched out, and I don't like it, I think she wants to sleep on the mattress. I don't open the door, but she comes in anyway carrying a bowl of soup. She sings a vague melody in a falsetto to words she's making up. When I see she's going, I feel like asking her something, but she's plugged into her Walkman headphones. Her chicken soup is a feeble imitation, a rice broth that slips painlessly down. There's a video game frozen on the television, Formula One cars on the starting grid. It's stopped bleeding down my gums, but the odd molar on the right side feels loose. I close my eyes and see diamonds. I can hear a raucous moan, but I don't know if it's mine.

SIX

The throbbing pain drags me out of bed early in the morning. I'd forgotten, and unthinkingly even forgiven, the previous night's clout. In retaliation to clemency, my face swelled up during the night and I woke up with a gelatinous mouth. I have to leave the room or I'll bang my head against the walls. I'm ready to throw a fit on the grass but the old man's snoring sucks me into the pantry. He's asleep, curled up naked among strips of rag, with a bottle of

Underberg stuck between folds of his skin, or the
rags. I grab the bottle. I walk across the kitchen,
and to get out, I have to use the door to push aside
the legs of the girl with the head of hair who's lying
on the flagstone floor; she's asleep listening to her
Walkman, singing quietly in the language of her
dreams.

Once outside I gargle with Underberg, and more
or less rouse myself for the new day. A red sky is
dawning, and a rancorous sun is on its way. I get rid
of the bottle when the old man wakes up bad-
tempered, and bellows out threatening to set the
house on fire. The kids burst out of the windows and
belt down the path to the orchard, tripping and shov-
ing each other. They bring back more limes than
they can get into their food-bags, and walk back spit-
ting at each other. I catch a lime that bounces down
the slope, and I get an urge to chase after the gang.
It was a stupid urge, as they all are, and I end up out
of breath on the flat ground by the empty pool.

Carrying a lime, alcohol burning my cheeks, I
cannot but think of my friend. I remember whole
days we spent together drinking *caipirinha* by the
edge of this pool. I have a clear memory of our last
afternoon on the farm, five years ago, he's sitting
right there, already half-groggy, slurring his speech.

He's looking at the horizon, smoothing his hair with his fingers, smoothing his sleek hair behind his ear, a gesture that, recalled now, seems to be copied from my sister. The day he made that gesture I didn't give it a second thought, there was certainly nothing else to it. But now besides the gesture, I see a glint in his eyes that troubles me. The glint must be a reflection of the horizon he was looking at, but the horizon isn't there in my memory, and his eyes glint for the sake of glinting.

My friend was drinking with me by the pool, and by that stage his conversation wasn't flowing. I think he was talking about Russian literature, but I'm not sure, because the words came out in a confused jumble and were lost. But my picture of him does get clearer and clearer: the gold chain in a tangle round his neck, the hairy mole just below his elbow, his ribs sticking out like a keyboard, his white trunks with three vertical green stripes. The only thing I can't remember is my friend's feet. We were always barefoot and I don't even remember seeing those feet. I never noticed if they were big or beautiful. I couldn't say if my friend had huge feet like the murdered gym teacher.

I again remember my friend looking at the horizon, his wet hair blacker than ever, which now he combs more slowly than before. Probably sensing he's being remembered, he makes the most of the situation. He takes a drag on a cigarette that didn't even exist in the previous memory; stays there letting himself be looked at like an actor in a profile. Who suddenly swings round towards me, wanting to take me by surprise with that glint in his eyes, which troubles me again. It'll soon be dark and I've still not got a look at his feet. But what you can't remember seeing one day, perhaps you can see later through some bias of memory. Perhaps by giving today's focus to that day's eyes. And that's how I finally see my friend's feet, out of a corner of memory's eye. I can see them but not what they're like; they're feet refracted in turbid water, impossible to gauge.

I imagine my friend receiving boys in his flat. My friend on his living-room sofa, drinking Campari and reading the boys poetry. His bare feet on the sofa, hidden under cushions, my friend smoothing his hair back behind his ear, and I imagine a boy getting annoyed at the whole scene. My friend opening up the album of French poets, as the boy cringes on the sofa. And the hatred filling him, making him suffer from another hatred, because he can't understand the double hatred overwhelming him, which comes both of great humiliation and contempt. I imagine the poetry being endless, and the boy going mad, looking for a clothesline or a kitchen knife, but that's all, my imagination runs dry, because my friend could never be a gym teacher. Once more I remember him next to me, looking at the horizon, his arms propped on the edge of the swimming pool, and my friend didn't even have biceps. I remember the moment he raised his glass, waved his empty glass with a slice of lime stuck to the bottom, and said he was going to recharge the *caipirinha*. He threatened to take his feet out, so I would get a close-up, as I did of the dead man's feet years later. Now I'm really disturbed by the idea of seeing my friend's feet, feet that I would watch naturally at that instant. But the instinctive gesture may be a reflex belonging to an intention from another time. And that afternoon I put my hand on his knee without knowing why, and said "No." I snatched the glass from him and went off to make a double *caipirinha*.

The alcohol that took my friend into poetry could also attack his nerves, make him aggressive. It was dark, and we were eating on the verandah when he decided I was a turd, no more no less. He said just that: "You're a turd." And told me I should imitate the Russian writer who renounced everything, dressed like a peasant, cooked his own rice, gave up his land and died in a railway station. He said I should also give up my land, even if it put me in dispute with my family, more turds. All existing laws and governments were equally turdish; my friend began to get worked up on the verandah, shouting out words, throwing plates and chairs into the patio, in a fit that soon brought out all the farm people. He exclaimed "Let the peasants come" and the peasants who came were the gardener, the man who looked after the horses, the old caretaker and his wife the cook, plus these people's sons and daughters, their daughters- and sons-in-law, and babes in arms. My friend shouted out several times "The land belongs to the peasants!" and these people thought it odd. Later on he quieted down, we threw our things into the boot of his car, a sedan on its last legs, and left the farm and a wide-open gate behind us.

I'll never forget that night because it ended in the city, in a penthouse near the beach, where some anthropology students were celebrating graduation. We didn't know anyone, and I don't know how we finished up there. Nor do I know who introduced me to one of the female anthropologists, who tried to teach me an African dance. She later told me she intended to get to know Egypt, spoke about her experience in films as a continuity girl, and at the end of the party she read the tarot cards for me. When my friend dropped me home, I still remember him saying he didn't think much of the anthropologist. I didn't argue; I never did argue with him. But before I went to sleep I lay thinking that he might not always get it right. I married the anthropologist a month after, lived shut up with her for four and a half years, and never heard any more of my friend.

"Clear off! Shoo! I told you to clear off!" the old caretaker comes and rails at the couple of toads on the bottom of the empty pool. The smaller toad, in the shallow end, keeps jumping up, hitting its feet against the sides, but it'll never make the edge. A more daring, skewed leap drops it in the deep end face to face with the fat toad, who already knows jumping anywhere doesn't help. And its golden eyes seem to follow the caretaker, climbing down the rickety ladder into the deep end, and striding confidently over that slimy surface. The fat toad seems indeed to know the old man, for it lifts its back up and puffs its head into double its size. The old man grabs the fat toad and hurls it into the distance. The small toad meanwhile has jumped into the shallow end and again started to smack its feet against the walls. The old man comes up the ramp on his knees and squats down in pursuit of the small toad. He's just about to seize it when it makes an impossible leap and reaches the edge. Soon after, however, as if elated by its record, it jumps backwards, reversing the parabola. The old man plucks the toad out of the air and throws it into the top of a mango tree.

I'm thinking how, when the redhead sells the jewels, my share will give me enough to live on for eight months, a year, even longer. Perhaps to travel, to visit Egypt, to go to Europe and into the subway where women wear jewels. But I'd prefer the redhead to delay clinching the deal. I quite like being suspended in time, counting the tiles in the pool, sucking the mangoes the old man brought me. At the end of the afternoon I leave the swimming pool, the three thousand, four hundred and fifty-six tiles, and find the old man again behind the orchard, right at the back of the farm, throwing stones into the banana grove and shouting "Clear off!"

I remembered the banana trees, but not such an exuberant cultivation. The banana grove covers the entire rear slope of the valley. In the straight tracks between the banana trees, they've planted bushes with sharp, stiff leaves, a kind of brownish-bronze spike at the extremities of its branches. Indifferent to the old man, men and women push the leaves aside and pick the blossom with oblique, furtive hands.

At dusk they limp up the hillside, the men carrying baskets on their shoulders and the women balancing them on their heads. They leave their load in the barn and rush out, limping even more. I can't work out how many there are, as they're walking in groups and all look equally thin and equally flaccid. They look away when they pass by me, but I still notice they've got white patches or clusters of warts on their skin. At a glance I can see some have got things wrong with their mouths, ears, noses, and one woman, who isn't that old, looks as if she's got a sponge rather than a face. They converge on the camp-site and hide away in their tents, two at a time. The tents switch on their music, trying to outdo each other, and the sound coming out is unbearable.

The kids with the limes run by, and I think it's time I also went down to the house. But when I reach the plank bridge, I find it's been taken over by three panting German shepherds. Past them stands one of the twins. He's smiling, but I don't know if it's the smile of one who gave me a glass of water, or one who smashed my face in. I swing round and walk up the dirt track not looking back, but aware I've got the foaming dogs at my heels, and the smiling twin restrains them with his breath. Each scrupulous step I take turns this into a long, exhausting march.

When I reach the gate, it's locked with a chain and padlock. Unthinkingly I start to shake it, and the chain rattling is the signal to attack. The dogs' teeth sink into my heel, my thigh and my arm, and a frayed voice calls out "Guso! Pordeval! Sussanha!" It's the shaven-headed kid, the brother of the girl with the head of hair. The two males run to lick his feet, but the bitch keeps her teeth in my wrist. I feel that if she wrenched her muzzle away, she'd rip the flesh off my hand like a glove. But the kid hits her over the skull with a bamboo stick, and she opens her mouth to yelp. The twin laughs and offers me a peppermint.

The kid and the German shepherds escort me silently down into the valley to the main house. Now and then I catch the sound of bamboo whipping the air. It's only the bamboo in the kid's hand that makes him a kid. Because he's got severe features and a bony face. And his jaw moves round, chewing relentlessly as if he had a mouth full of stones.

I go into the kitchen, taking care not to wake anyone. The only light in the house comes from the pantry. As I go past, I can see the old man and the girl with the head of hair opposite each other, she's on the stool and he's on a pile of rags. The old man's hand is round his hard prick. Granddaughter is smiling at Granddad's hard prick. It's a solid, pink, gleaming prick that I don't think matches his veiny hand. It doesn't look like the old man's prick, more a prick to go with the logo-crazy nylon windcheater the old man's wearing. The girl now turns on me the same smile she was directing at the prick. Then she gets serious and stands up. She walks past me and over to her brother, who's waving a cassette tape at her. She sticks the cassette into her Walkman, puts on her headphones and walks round and round the kitchen, in a knee-length T-shirt bearing the imprint of a politician's face.

I spend the rest of the night tossing in bed, thinking I can hear a telephone ringing in the distance. Im-

possible to sleep with a telephone ringing endlessly
in the distance. Day breaks, and I think the telephone's still ringing. It must be almost midday when
I imagine my mother answers the phone. She will
answer her way, mute, waiting for someone to say
"Hello!" The redhead will say "Hello! Hello! Hello!"
and my mother will hang up because she doesn't
recognise the voice that's neither male nor female.
Then the redhead will dial my sister's number, and
her butler will answer that madam can't be disturbed. The redhead will insist that the matter is in
madam's interest, it's a delicate matter, it concerns
madam's brother. The butler will knock on my sister's door, and she'll be walking round and round
her bedroom in a silk peignoir. Her husband will be
stretched out on the bed in sports gear and Italian
shoes, pretending to read a report, but eyeing my
sister's movements. She will seem fed up about
something, and bend over to squash down in the ash-
tray a cigarette she has just lit. The butler will knock
harder and they'll both chorus "What is it?" The
butler will barely begin to speak and they'll both get
it wrong; they'll think it's me on the phone. My sister
will say I should ring back later and her husband will
say that's enough of giving me money. She'll light
another cigarette, fed up about something.

I'm already asleep when I hear the telephone again, and this time I imagine the redhead tells the butler it's a matter of life and death. Or he'll say that madam's brother's head is on the block. The butler will knock again, but my brother-in-law will have already gone out and my sister won't listen. My sister will be in the shower in a bathroom I'm unfamiliar with, and it would be a pyramid lined with mirrors. At a single glance it would be possible to see my sister from every angle. And the vision would be so instantaneous that every image of her would fuse in the retina of whoever looked. And to see so much of her at the same time, front and back, and side, and above, and below in a single image, would perhaps be like seeing nothing, but it would be to have seen her absolute.

One more telephone call and the redhead will hand over to one of the twins who gets straight to the point; he'll say if they don't come up with the goods, the duchess's brother'll get lead between the eyes. The butler will stand there scared stiff and helpless since his master is on the air shuttle and madam has just left without having her breakfast, no one knows where, driving herself with wet hair.

·   ·   ·

I wake up not knowing if I slept too little or too much. It's mid-afternoon, but I don't know what day it is. I jump through the window and leave by the verandah, on the side opposite the kitchen. I don't want to bump into the old man or anyone else. There's no one in the harvest area. I walk by the side of the banana plantation down a path I know that joins the stream on the high ground. It's a path my father loved to walk, which everybody avoids because of the snakes. Just there a big stone divides the waters of the stream, and when the stream's not full it's an easy crossing point. I then climb up through the shadows on the hillside and reach the gate without touching the dirt track. Intending to jump the gate, I accelerate and gather up strength; when I reach it, it's open. The coast's clear and I could easily leave the farm, but now I just feel like going back to bed. I slowly retrace my steps along the track, stop in front of the guest-house, and everything is deserted. In the repair shop, the same cars, bikes, engines, chassis, plus the zero-kilometre van painted swimming-pool blue. Behind the shed, the convoy of trailers and the dappled cow. Inside the biggest trailer a telephone rings and rings and rings and no one answers.

An old car with its exhaust loose drives on to the

farm. A rickety truck blows up dust as it speeds through the gate. A black-and-white truck banging along the dirt track, and it's the police. On the one hand, I want to throw myself in their path, wave my arms and shout "I'm here!" On the other, I want to plunge into the bamboo thicket and that's what I do. I see the police van head towards the stream, pass the camp-site and manoeuvre forward, then reverse and park against the barn. I scramble down the hill-side holding on to the bamboo, in time to see the ex-boxer leave the steering-wheel and the redhead get out the other side. The ex-boxer opens the rear door and it's the shaven-headed kid who leaps out of the cage, followed by the twins, who put two bricks under the rear wheels. They all rush away from the van as if it was going to explode. All except for the kid, who whistles his way into the barn and soon emerges accompanied by the limping harvesters. They are carrying bulky green canvas bags that they unload into the back of the van. They fill up the space, close the door with difficulty and put the surplus sacks on the bonnet, obstructing the windscreen. Then they limp back to the camp-site, but there's no music today; instead of going into the tents, they start taking them down.

The ex-boxer returns to the steering-wheel, and

drives off, leaning his head out, with the redhead as
a co-driver. Each twin hangs on a running board,
holds the sacks on the bonnet, and the kid rushes
behind. The twins jump off at the repair shop with
the bags from the bonnet, and the van splutters off
out of the farm.

I walk down to the main house and sit on the edge of
the verandah, with my back to my bedroom window.
I can feel in my skin the approach of night. It's still
light over the rest of the farm, but I'm breathing in
the night air. On the trees I see in the light of day
the movement of the leaves has already changed and
it's a nocturnal movement; as certain smells and
noises are nocturnal, as there are nocturnal animals
and flowers that don't open by day, and thoughts so
clear they can only be seen at night. The girl with
the head of hair is nocturnal; and when I come to
myself, she's braiding my hair. Then she sits beside
me and starts pedalling into empty space under the
verandah. I notice her eyes are very round as if per-
manently surprised. She rests her small hand on my
thigh and her fingers are short like a paw's. She puts
her earphones on and sings "Hmmmmmmmmmmm,"

a song without words. To reach the top notes, she tightens her grip, and even bruises me. And as I begin to understand the melody, she takes her hand off my thigh and presses stop. She disappears so suddenly I almost feel robbed.

It's a starry night, and I see before I hear the gourd-coloured jeep on the plank-bridge. On this side of the bridge there is a very bendy stretch of dirt track for whoever drives down to the main house. But the jeep prefers to cut down the steep slope, and bounces into the yard, and is about to climb on to the verandah, and brakes against my kneecaps. A twin jumps off and pulls out the grey suitcase that was on the back seat. First I thought it was my old suitcase, the one stowed in the sentry-box at my sister's, but it's not, it's a bit bigger, and has a soft, bulging cover. When it's opened on the verandah, it gives off a smell of banana that doesn't convince me—it's exaggerated. In fact, as soon as the twin starts removing the banana leaves from the top of the case, I feel that it's another essence. The suitcase is stuffed with a kind of brownish-bronze spike, dry but smooth, pressed and tangled into a crude dough. It's a suitcase stuffed with marihuana. The twin says "Juicy joints" and covers up the grass with the banana leaves, like someone tucking in a baby. He shuts the case and signals to me to get into the jeep.

Before dropping me and the case at the bus-stop, the twin says the boss liked my face. And that his twin brother, who knows the market better, told the boss this suitcase contained twice the value of the jewels. But he says that he knows the boss better and can guarantee that if I produce some equally choice pieces, the boss will be ready to pay out two suitcases. But he adds that he and his twin are of the opinion that if I don't want to get really worked over, I'd better spend some time in another neck of the woods.

The Brialuz service station is shut and I feel a bit cold. A few trucks have stopped there and people must be sleeping in the cabs. Someone's smoking next to a tyre with a sign painted in white letters: 24-HOUR TYRE REPAIR SERVICE. A man in overalls comes out of the lavatory and stands looking up at the sky. I cross the road and lean against the lamp-post, which is the stop for the bus that goes down the mountains. Later I sit on the case, which gives under me, and one of the locks opens and lets the banana smell escape.

SEVEN

It's daylight, 6 a.m., and just a skinny character in a check shirt with me at the stop as the bus emerges from over the hill. But it no sooner comes to a halt than kids with bags of limes spring from every corner. They climb on the bumper, stick their feet on the windows and settle down on the bus roof in a luggage rack that seems made for them. The steep steps make it difficult for me to get in at the front, and the suitcase I'm pushing up with my thighs gets jammed against the driver's gear lever. Check Shirt takes advantage of this to get ahead of me, pay his ticket and sit down next to someone even skinnier. I push the case along the aisle, thinking it could burst open at any moment. There's only half a place next to a fat black woman with the face of a good cook, since her left buttock occupies half of my seat.

And here are the bends again and the kids swaying from one side to the other of the luggage rack, going "Whoooooo." The rest of the passengers seem used to it, and even I think it's normal to look out of the window on my right and see the head of a five-year-old hanging down. The inverted grimace, blood-red, eyes me, its arms gesticulating like someone with an urgent message. The kid starts to bash the panels of the bus until the cook opens her window, and he says "Get this pot smell!" He disappears as if he had slid to the top, and then they start tap-dancing on the roof of the bus. And new ruddy grimaces start appearing at the twenty windows, and fingers prodding the glass, pointing at me and the suitcase.

For the rest of the journey I look down like someone in search of religion. I concentrate on my crossed hands, open my fingers up one by one, close all five at once, open them in reverse order, and am only interrupted by the frightened cook next to me, slapping the window and making the sign of the cross, her eyes out of their sockets. I recognise by their limp the harvesters along the roadside. We pass them quite slowly, because we're going round a dangerous bend behind a tank truck. They hide their faces with their radios, record-players, amplifiers, loudspeakers, and the rolled-up tents the men carry on their shoulders and the women balance on their heads. A fresh tap-dance on the bus roof, and the kids shout out in chorus "Look at the E.T.'s! Look at the E.T.'s!"

When we hit a straight stretch of road near the suburbs, the kids get the idea of racing down the luggage rack. But a sudden brake hurls them at least two of them into space. I see two bodies whirling round like propellers in front of the bus, floppy dolls beating their arms and tap-dancing in the void. Until they halt in mid-air like insects hurtling against the window, and the fall is instantaneous, impossible to see. I hear a bump right under my feet, and even think I see something roll along the hard shoulder.

The bus picks up speed, and the rest of the jour-ney proceeds more calmly. The kids jump out in the

bus station with the bus still moving, and buzz off
with their bundles. I let the fat cook go by, wait for
the bus to empty, but when I get off with my case,
the kids rush up the platform to me like a welcoming
committee. They follow me out of the station, get in
the way, sniff at my case, all in a station awash with
police.

I grab the first taxi and tell the driver to head for
the south of the city. With only his left hand on the
wheel, he sits sideways to the traffic, speaking to me
in the back seat. He talks and chews three mushy
matchsticks, and is wearing a shirt a size too small,
its short sleeves rolled up as if he's about to be vac-
cinated. He relates the incident of the married passenger he left at the station, who had no money for
her fare. Shows off the passenger's work number
that's scribbled on a cigarette packet. I look at the
meter that is never still, look at the price tariff covered in plastic inside the glove compartment, wondering how much is left from the hand-out at my
sister's party. I say "Just here" at the end of the
tunnel and put what I've got in the driver's palm. I
get out quickly but he shouts "Come on, your lord-
ship!" opening the boot up and pointing at my case
as if smelling something that didn't appeal.

The nearest place I know to the mouth of the tunnel is my mother's house. I reckon she won't be upset if I leave the case for a while in one of her wardrobes. In the middle room where Mummy never sets foot, there's a wall-length wardrobe containing my father's things, white uniforms, tartan suits, woollen overcoats, dinner-jacket, summer jacket, some German brogues I even tried to inherit, but they were too big. If I slip the suitcase into that wardrobe, Mummy will never know. Obviously any day she could wake up in a state, decide on a general spring clean, need to air all the rooms, and by chance open the wardrobe she's forgotten, full of clothes that no longer existed for her. Perhaps she'll think those outfits ridiculous, the ceremonial uniform, all these suits in the same pattern, perhaps she'll think Dad ridiculous. Perhaps she'll work up a rage, call the porter, and order him to throw everything into the incinerator, the suitcase included. Perhaps she'll feel pity and decide to donate it all to some charity shop, and the Sisters will be taken aback by that horrific case among the spoils from my father. I imagine the case being opened up in the cloisters, the semicircle of Carmelite nuns contemplating the lump. By this time I'm at my mother's address, walking between green marble columns of a once sumptuous edifice by the sea.

The porter's willing because he wants to carry my case, wants to run and open the lift for me, wants to call me "young master" and say the good son returns home. A black who's almost blue, though losing his lustre of late, he was already white-haired thirty years ago. He always wears the same striped waistcoat, so he looks like a slave in a film. He walks very slowly, suffers from arthritis and is always happy with his lot. He once bought a radio and began to listen to variety programmes, the kind where people talk about everything with an echo in their voices. It was a powerful set, blared out from the hallway, down the lift-shaft and round the whole building. One night my dad went down to the street to look for me, and was already in a temper when he came down because when he got home he expected everyone to be indoors: "One of these days I'll bolt the door when I come in!" Dragging me by the scruff of the neck, crossing the hallway for the third time in a row, as the announcer read out the horoscope, my dad told the porter to switch that rubbish off. And said he'd never heard of a servant switching on to astrology, let alone blacks, who don't even have stars. The porter thought it really funny. He sold his radio and went around for months laughing and repeating "Blacks don't have stars, blacks don't have stars."

Before I ring the bell, I try to spy on my mother's movements. If she's in her bedroom, no point in ringing, for she won't hear. But by this time she must be up, she's already washed her face, heated the milk, mixed it with oats, and it's more likely she's on her *chaise-longue* in the lounge, reading a fashion magazine. But even if she's dragging her feet past the door, coughing and complaining, I think I won't notice anything from outside. The door to her flat is a block of heavy dark jacaranda, with a big rosette carved in the centre of a pattern of diamonds. When they brought the coffin lid to my father's wake, I even imagined it was the door.

And Mummy's probably asleep over the magazine on her lap, indifferent to the new collections. She may be dreaming again about the man in gloves in the hanging theatre, that's Father because he's six feet tall and leans backwards as he walks, but it isn't Father because he speaks in a strange accent and has got the face of a sheep. After a certain age I think our stock of dreams dries up and it's all re-peats. But as nothing's totally detestable, old people's power of recall fades as well, so they're not sure if they dreamed a dream or not. They recognise the high points and say "That's right," but aren't sure what's coming next. And if what comes next is a precipice, a fire, an air disaster, the death of all their relatives, a chase round a labyrinth, a cataclysm that makes one wake up frightened, gasping for air, shout out, sit up in bed, become sleepless, the old people say "I knew that" or "Didn't I tell you?" And back to another dream with no great expectations, but no greater boredom, preferring to dream all the dreams again than to answer the door bell. In fact I don't know if I managed to ring the bell, but I've already decided not to bother my mother. Sooner or later she'll have to open the door, in the hope of a letter from abroad or one of those magazines she subscribes to. When she finds the case, she'll call the porter on the intercom, and he'll say the case is mine, straighten his waistcoat, come up and put it wherever Mummy wants it kept.

From the seafront promenade on the other side of the avenue, looking over a royal poinciana, I can see my mother's eighth-floor flat. But she'd never come to the window. People who live facing the sea don't appear at their windows. The windows are always shut because of the sea breeze that rusts the metal, and to maintain the air-conditioning. These people put lined curtains behind the windows, and the façades along the beach are all dressed up with inside-out curtains. In the more modern buildings the architects have created terraces to imitate decks, terraces that are littered with wicker or fibreglass furniture and flower pots with ferns or areca palms. But the people in the modern buildings also keep away from their terraces.

Suppose Mummy won't open her door today. Suppose tomorrow a letter comes from Spain and the porter goes up and balances it lengthwise between the mat and the door as Mummy recommends. When he sees the case he'll get confused, and end up ringing the bell, against all instructions. Nobody will answer and he'll go down and sleep with it buzzing round his head. Early next morning he'll go back up, see the case lying down and the letter standing up, ring the bell again and again and try to force the door open which, besides the bolt, now has a safe-deposit-style security lock. Finally he'll ring the police station who'll send a patrol car with two policemen who'll remove the case, letter and mat and sniff under the door, asking people to be careful with matches. The fire brigade will turn up to force an entry, but the chief will prefer to get permission from the ninth floor to get in down through the window. With a cloth over his nose he'll open the door from the inside, and the porter will have to put up with a crowd of firemen and policemen rushing down the living room, banging against the *chaise-longue*, advancing down the corridor, invading my mother's bedroom, flinging the windows open and thumping on the bathroom door. An obese sergeant will throw himself against the door, taking it with him on to the wash-basin, and the axe-wielding chief will leap over the sergeant. When the windows are shattered, police and firemen will stop for a moment in the doorway and all look the same way, but the porter won't make out what they can see in the bath.

They'll clear a path for a fellow in a crumpled suit who won't stay long inside. He'll order the porter to come with him into the living room, where he'll ask after any relative of the victim who could be informed about the occurrence. The porter will say the widow came from a good, well-connected family, and that won't interest the inspector. Then he'll say he's got the eldest daughter's telephone number in his desk-drawer in the lobby, and that will satisfy the inspector. Anxiously the porter will add that there's also a son and look at the case behind the door furtively. But as he's a man with a vice of purity, he can't look furtively at the case; first he'll look at the case and then furtively at the inspector. Enough to give everything away. The case that could have stayed there innocent, odourless and out of the way, will be set out in the living room by a policeman and its contents turned over in the presence of the inspector and the firemen. The odour flooding out will smother all traces of gas in the flat.

EIGHT

I was on the beach looking out to sea, the sea, the sea vomiting sea, and now it's not easy to cross back over the avenue. I know it's just past midday because there's an equally dense flow of traffic in both directions. I'm stuck for ten or twenty minutes on the central bollard next to a sign advertising cigarettes and a broken digital, its unfinished numbers looking like a strange alphabet. I reach and rattle the wrought-iron gate outside my mother's block, and the porter comes over, walking quickly, and arriving slowly like a clockwork doll. I go up to the eighth floor where my suitcase is still lying flat on its back. I push it over to the lift with my feet. For some reason or other I jam the suitcase against the sliding door, press violently down on my mother's bell and run into the lift. As he sees me come down with the suitcase, it's on the tip of the porter's tongue to say "The young master's just back from his travels and off already?" when the intercom rings on his table. He answers and I can almost hear my mother's voice complaining about the non-stop ring of her broken bell. The porter says nothing, only nods, does it with such solicitude that it must reach up above. He switches off and says "Dr. Lastriglianza on the third floor saw the mouse." He pulls at the hem of his striped waistcoat, and goes up in the service lift. I stay some twenty to forty minutes all alone in the lobby, looking at the intercom, thinking it will ring again.

I walk off down the shop-filled streets, switching my suitcase from hand to hand at each new block. When they're both raw flesh, I try to carry the case in my arms like a nurse carrying an old man. It gives me some relief but I can't see where I'm going. I stop on the corner of two treeless avenues and de-

cide to enter a glass-fronted shop that I took for a
sweetshop but is really the branch of a bank. As I
set foot inside despite the cool air, I sense I might
have made a wrong move. Right in the entrance is a
security guard inside a steel capsule, his eyes bobbing like a couple of fish behind the visor. The two
armed sentries on the corner I thought were traffic
police also belong to the bank. More foolhardy than
entering a bank with this case would be to turn round
and head out; the men drifting casually in and out
carry fine leather briefcases or James Bond attaché
cases. All I can do is sit down on the corner of a sofa,
on the carpeted mezzanine floor where there are var-
ious people with envelopes on their laps, as if they
expect something to happen.

I sit down opposite a girl I think I know though I
can't remember from where. She also looks at me,
but doesn't greet me, doesn't smile at me, rather
seems to have damp eyes. When I see the crutches
leaning against the sofa arm, I realise it's the sister
of an acquaintance of mine, the one who gave parties
in a house surrounded by almond trees. She keeps
looking at me without greeting me, and I can't understand why she's decided to cry in a bank. True
she is paralysed, but that's been true for some time,
I think she got polio when she was fifteen. In the

heyday of parties, in her twenties, she must have already become resigned, but the fact is I never stopped to think how she felt. It stands to reason that she never used to make an appearance in the main lounge. I couldn't guess she went up to her room, left her door half-open, put out the light, and sat out of sight watching us. Perhaps she cried the whole of Saturday, admiring the party but unable to dance. And no one will know whether she slammed her door at midnight, moaned in bed, and how the more she sunk her head into the bolster, the more she heard the dudum-dudum-dudum of the double bass. It's clear that today, as she looks at me, she remembers those parties and may feel like crying again.

A man says "Nineteen," and, digging her crutches into the carpet, she pulls herself up like a gymnast on the horizontal bar. She's got very wide shoulders, but otherwise her body seems well built. She's wearing long trousers and I imagine her legs will always be fifteen years old. She walks by me and my eyes follow her, seeing movements where there can't be any, but where the shadows of a movement are still at play; or perhaps it's a fictitious movement she has learned the art of suggesting. Before she sits down with the manager, she turns round, red-eyed, red-faced, her neck flushed. I look the other way, and stare at the window which the striplighting in the bank and a column behind have turned into a mirror. It's so long since I looked in a mirror that it takes me for someone else.

After a brief consultation with the manager she leaves the bank and I leave too. No policeman in the world would grab hold of the suitcase of someone accompanying a cripple. The difficulty is to keep pace with her crutches, me handicapped by the case I'm now carrying on my back. She's a bold little woman, crosses the road without looking, and cars that never stopped at a red light brake to let her over. I'm left behind, and hardly identify the building she enters. But it's a building covered in blue tiles, half of which have come away, where she must live with her brother. When her brother sees her come tearfully in, he'll understand the loan has been refused. Irritated by capitalism, he'll say can't think why banks exist if they don't free up money to a lame customer. Feeling tortured, she'll whisper he's entirely to blame, he got into debt by giving party after party. He'll say "All right, all right," on the point of throwing in her face bills for imported medicines, not to mention that physiotherapy that doesn't help at all. Reading as always her brother's thoughts, she'll say the medical treatment comes out of her savings and that they had to sell the house with the almond trees in order to cope with the parties. He'll say "All right, all right," thinking about the house with the almond trees. Her voice will get thinner and she'll say it was humiliating enough moving to a two-roomed flat, in the worst building in the neighbourhood, its tiles falling off while he's giving three parties a week. He'll say "All right, all right," thinking about the launch of the bed-sitter.

My friend lives two blocks past the tiled building in this same treeless avenue. His is a dingy and honest building that has come to an agreement with time. Its rough façade will always be the same, because the owners are dead, the tenants have obscure contracts, and the contractors gave up on pulling it down. It's a building on three floors which few people notice, and those who do wouldn't like to live there, but the people who do live there say they'll only leave for the cemetery. On the front wall remain the words "Conenal Buldng" with the brass letters still stuck to the cement facing. The consensus is it was baptised "Continental," except for the old couple who've been living there since they were married; she's positive the building was called "Confidential" at the time and he remembers it clearly as the "Count Reginald Building."

After five years, you still have to open the door from the inside by slipping your hand through a hole in the broken glass. In his room at the rear of the ground floor, the concierge doesn't miss a Reverend Azea programme, even less now it's on TV. There's no lift, and the light on the stairs goes out a minute after it's switched on. In one minute I used to reach the third floor, but today, with the suitcase, supporting its handle with the joints of my fingers, the blackout catches me before I'm up the first flight. There's no switch halfway up the stairs, and the case seems to weigh double in the dark. By the first floor, I'm thinking I'll ask my friend for help. I switch on the light.

My friend had been looking for me after I got married, but I never knew what he wanted. He got my telephone number, and I now remember him ringing at times my ex-wife considered inconvenient. She answered and said I was at work, night-duty, but he didn't seem to believe her. He'd ring back ten minutes later, and my ex-wife always beat me to the

phone. And if anything wound her up, it was saying
"Hello," and not getting an answer from the other
end. At times I thought it could be my mother, but
she swore it wasn't, it was always him, it was his
silence. My ex-wife, who already had a real dislike
for my friend, came to hate the phone. Whenever it
rang, she would say "Let it ring, it's that man
again." In bed she asked me what the man wanted
from me, but I couldn't know, I never answered the
phone. And when she decided once and for all to
take the phone off its hook, I thought it was a good
decision. I switch on the light.

I need to carry this case to the top by myself. As
soon as he opens the door, I intend to push it inside
and go down without saying a word. He'll stand there
for some time looking at the case, a couple of hours
looking at that amorphous suitcase, and will probably conclude I've returned some books. That's it, the
poets, the novels, or the philosophy, the universal
history, the atlas, the encyclopaedia, who can tell
how many volumes returned five years overdue,
hence my shamefaced retreat. As he no longer remembers the books he lent me, my friend will open
the case with a nostalgic curiosity, as if he's opening
an inheritance from himself. The macerated banana

leaves will pop out, and underneath them the marihuana. His first reaction will be one of repugnance,
but not at the marihuana, at the unexpected. Just as
you find repugnant the consistency of something
you've put into your mouth by mistake. My friend
will close the case straightaway, but the idea of the
marihuana will linger on outside. And when he opens
the case a second time, he'll do it with the reverse of
curiosity; he'll open it caressing it inside, enjoying
the slow discovery of something that's already wide
open.

I switch on the light and attack the next flight. I'm
stimulated by the idea of the case being in good
hands. I imagine it open on the living-room floor, my
friend listening to the classics, his visitors helping
themselves, and before a month's out I bet he'll be
on the track of my new address. He can even ask
after me at my ex-wife's boutique. Perhaps he'll ring
my mother's house at some inconvenient time, but I
know he'll never find me any more.

The time-switch runs out on me two steps from
the second floor; here it's not totally dark, because
of a thin ray of light from the hallway. As well as the
smell of garlic through a door that's ajar and a woman's voice singing "I think of the bad times, the bad

times to come . . ." She breaks off her song, and I'm afraid she's heard a noise. But she soon remembers the words and picks up the thread again ". . . I know you despise me, and I can bear it no more."

I walk across the half-lit landing, up the last flight unable to discern anything, and come to a halt on the eighth or ninth stair. It's an unpleasant step on the curve which won't take the whole case. It hangs there, a dead-weight, and I feel my fingers wanting to let go of the handle. But I've already one foot on the third floor, and I believe it will obey a last tug. When I'm in the air, I don't know if it was the case that pulled me so furiously, or if I was bowled over by someone rushing downstairs. I hit my right cheek against the sharp edge of a step, and hear the case rumbling downstairs, as if it was in hot pursuit of someone. The woman who was singing opens the door and the band of light turns into a spotlight on the case that's fallen into two pieces. She's a short-ish Indian woman with a scarf round her head, who's crouching down to sniff the grass that's scattered around. Then she scrambles downstairs, returns to switch the light back on, scrambles downstairs not noticing me stretched out just above her landing. She must bump into the concierge who was coming upstairs, because they both start arguing on the first floor. On the third floor I think I can hear jets of voice, like a man without the strength to cry fully. I lever myself up on to my elbows; my face is bleeding and it's difficult to prise it from the stone. The concierge and the Indian woman come upstairs arguing, and I go in through the kitchen door she left open. There's a garlicky gravy on the fridge, and onion rings burnt at the edges. The Indian woman and caretaker are now arguing about the suitcase; he asks if it fell from heaven, and she saw when it was thrown down. They go up another flight, and I leave the kitchen, take a double jump over the case and skid on the marihuana. Caretaker and Indian are shouting on the third floor; I don't know if it's an argument, since they seem to be parallel shouts. As I walk down the last step, a voice on the ground floor begs for mercy, but it's Reverend Azea preaching.

I leave the building, and suddenly it's pitch-dark; I imagine a day that switches off each minute. I lean on the pebble-dashed wall, scrape my back as I slide to the ground, my head between my legs. Transformed into a sea shell, I hear distant voices, think I hear sirens. When I get up, I may be seeing things clearer than they are. I see a gangling black emerge from the other end of the avenue. He's jay-walking, swaying through the traffic jam, and he's wearing rubber briefs in a jaguar-skin pattern. He walks by me with a stupid smile on his face. He's about to enter my friend's building, peeling an orange with a penknife.

The police car tries so hard to break its way through that it knots up the traffic. Its siren seems more like publicity as it sings and blares out without budging. The pavement can't take so many people flocking there from nearby streets, and they don't like to see me advancing from the opposite direction. I can see the crowd blocking all my paths, but in reality I am the one who is getting in their way. I walk along squashed against the walls until ejected through the loose door in a hoarding.

I'm now in the grounds of a house in course of demolition. The works are at a standstill and the rubble is piled up at the back. By climbing up the rubble, I reach the top of the wall behind a state school. I jump down into the playground, and land next to a fellow in a polo-neck, who's smoking and leaning against the wall. The fellow says nothing; looks at me, then at his watch, as if he's been expecting me for some time. He walks out with me,

and perhaps he's a teacher smoking on the sly to
avoid setting a bad example. He accompanies me
down the side of the school, close to the classroom
windows, and some pupils think our heads look
funny. I leave the school, go round the corner, and
so does he. He's smoking non-filter cigarettes he
taps on his watch and then lights with his dog-end. I
can't make out how he's not choking in that woollen
sweater pulled up to his neck.

If I decided to run, he'd never catch me. I could
rush into the garage of one of these buildings, and
down a road out the other side. But when he stops at
the shop to buy cigarettes, for some reason I wait
outside. I begin to get used to his tacit company; it's
a bit like walking with one of the family, a much
older brother, or a young uncle. We go into a shopping mall. The shop where my ex-wife works doesn't
have a sign outside, but I can make it out in the
distance. I can see the owner of the boutique in the
entrance and I don't know if she saw me, because
she turns round and goes inside.

They have shut the boutique door. My ex-wife is
sitting on the carpet, her back to the window, sorting
clothes out. She opens her arms, pulls out a silk
shawl with her fingertips and throws it in the air.

The shawl settles like a butterfly, but she's not satisfied and repeats the exercise. My ex-wife has this
habit of sitting on the floor with her legs doubled
outwards in a W, which I've tried to imitate and got
cramp. She's wearing a bun, and the hair on her
neck is thinner, fairer than the rest, and curly. I feel
it will stand on end if I blow lightly. I tap on the
window, but she keeps struggling with the shawl.
The pale-faced shop assistant comes and goes with
some coathangers and seems to want to make a point
of not seeing me. He passes some clothes over to my
ex-wife, averting his gaze as if handing a towel to a
bashful woman in the bath. The boutique owner is
going over the accounts behind the counter. Her
eyes are getting dim, but she doesn't want to wear
glasses, so she stands back from the cash book,
looking rather distrustful.

I ring the bell I've just spotted by the side of the
door, and hear nothing. The windows must be
soundproofed, for the boutique owner is saying
something to my wife and I can't hear that either.
Now it's the teacher whom I'd forgotten who's ringing the bell. No reactions inside, but it's not possible
the bell's out of order. It's still business hours and in
no way should the door be locked. I decide to keep

my finger on the bell until something happens. What happens is that the owner closes the book, slams it down on the table and picks up the red phone. My ex-wife jumps up, puts her hand on the owner's hand, and manages to dissuade her from calling the police. When the owner hangs up, the teacher's finger is on the bell. I pull his arm, and he goes slightly off balance. He looks at his watch, lights his cigarette with another, starts off up the escalator.

I was going after the teacher when I saw a big-buttocked woman, wearing a tunic, walk up and into the shop. I run back but they've bolted the door again. I ring the bell, and only the big-buttocked customer looks at me. I start rattling the door, and suddenly there's an explosion. The boutique owner shrieks, the customer sways, the pale shop assistant lifts up a coathanger and my ex-wife runs to the red telephone. It was the reinforced glass door that exploded, shattering into little piles of bluish glass on the doorstep and in my hair. My ex-wife dials three digits, and talks quietly, her hand over her mouth and the mouthpiece. No more door, but I no longer want to go inside. I've forgotten what I wanted to suggest to my ex-wife.

I leave and peep in the other shop-fronts. At the

foot of the escalator I meet the teacher coming down
from the mezzanine. But now he doesn't keep in step
with me; he stops when I walk, walks when I stop,
goes in and out of a stationery shop with swing-
doors. I see a white van with white windows park by
the pavement opposite the shopping mall, with the
inscription ECNALUBMA on the hood, and "Dr Ber-
doch's Sanatorium" on the doors. A big male nurse
gets out smiling and opens his arms to the teacher.
The latter looks at his watch, lets himself be hugged,
and gets in the car with the nurse.

I'm making up my mind which way to go when a
heavy hand comes down on my shoulder and makes
my collar-bone go crack. I imagine it's another
nurse, but it's an even bigger fellow, beige-jacketed
and lavender-scented; it must be the security guard
from the shopping mall, because he starts to frisk
me. A black car with black windows backs up where
the ambulance was, and gives seven short, rhythmic
blasts on its horn. The security guard forgets me and
goes to deal with the horn. He has to twist round to
hear the woman in the back of the car, and stands
there with his rump in the air. The driver gets out to
open the rear door so I can get in.

NINE

My sister's skinny friend is bent down on the seat, her head stuck in a tennis bag she's ferreting around in with both hands. She says "Hello," and something else I can't make out in a muffled voice. She's wearing a white pleated skirt, and her thighs are just slightly thicker than her legs, but no cellulite. When the car enters the tunnel, I see it was a Tampax she was looking for in her bag. In spite of the dark I see her undo the Tampax and soak it in perfume that she pours out of a tear-shaped bottle. As we leave the tunnel, she starts to apply the scented cotton wool to the right side of my face. It absorbs the splinters of glass that fell from my hair and lodged in the open wounds in their path. There's more glass than I thought, because when she screws it up the cotton wool crunches.

The chauffeur makes an illegal turn, goes down a temporary viaduct, drives along private roads, and to my surprise we're climbing the slopes that lead to my sister's condominium. In no way am I going to my sister's house. I look at my skinny companion, and now she has her mouth shut, her lips clammed tight, the mouth of a vindictive woman. It may be she's remembered the other night, when she grabbed me on my way out of the closet, and I deserted her in the penumbra. Perhaps she's going through an age crisis, and that memory will be torturing her more and more as the car lumbers up the hillside. She'll chivvy the driver, tell him to turn the air-conditioning on to maximum. She'll look at the roof, at the driver's topknot, look through the almost opaque window, lower her eyes. She'll bring her knees together, and hate having two thighs that don't touch even when she's sitting down. She'll open up the cotton wool, and feel like putting each splinter back in my blood. I reckon when we go into the house my sister will see her friend's face and say "Well, sweetie, what's got into you?" And then the skinny woman will avert her gaze and point at me; unable to condemn me for disregarding her, she'll become cross-eyed and denounce me as a jewel thief.

I get ready to jump out as soon as we're level with the guard-post, but the guard recognises the black car from a distance and opens the main gate in advance. I could throw myself on the skinny woman, suck her lips and inflict a wet kiss upon her. I could slip my hand up her skirt, quickly do it all right there, but the driver roars up through the condominium like a madman, tyres screeching, horn blasting, and into the garden of number 16, making the lawn bristle.

The skinny woman grabs the racquet from behind the headrest, and hops out and over to the tennis court. I'm right behind, with the bag that she forgot on the seat. I deduce she couldn't have seen the jewels in my pockets that night. I even think she didn't see where I came from. That night perhaps she didn't even have a clue as to whom she was clinching. She walks round the pool to get to the court, and anyone harbouring a serious accusation doesn't skip like that.

My brother-in-law's playing the ball against the wall along one side of the court. Over his shorts he's wearing a mustard-coloured polo shirt with an alligator on the left side. He comes over and kisses the skinny woman twice by the net, while giving me a kind of military salute. The skinny woman asks "Has she rung?" and he says "No." The skinny woman says "She's bound to ring today," and he says "I doubt it." My brother-in-law's put on several kilos in a few days, he's out of breath, and rests an arm on the skinny woman's shoulder. He looked sunburned, but close up it's more like a therapeutic tan. The skinny woman says "In the airport I thought she looked megadistressed." She pinches the blue crocodile on his shirt with her nails and says "But she'll get over it quickly abroad." They take up positions on the court and lazily knock the ball around. I take it my sister's gone on a trip. The night before, packing her suitcases, she certainly went after her jewels. It's getting dark, and the floodlights switch on automatically.

The game's about to begin. My brother-in-law

throws the ball in the air with one hand, and with the other unleashes his serve, bellowing out as if he'd been thumped in the stomach. The ball hits the net. On his second serve he doesn't bellow, only twitches his mouth, and the ball spins up as it bounces to the other side. The skinny woman grips her racquet with both hands, crosses her legs and hits the ball in the direction of my brother-in-law, who returns the ball to the back of the court and runs to the net. I thought the skinny woman wouldn't get there in time, but she does and, wielding her racquet like a scythe, lifts the ball high in the air. My brother-in-law raises his racquet neck-high preparing a smash, but is deceived by the curve, runs backwards, off-balance, his body going faster than his legs, the skinny woman shouts "Oh shit!" as his backbone hits the wire fence. He walks back to serve from the left, and wastes time staring at his racquet, pinches the strings. I throw him the ball which rolled near me, but he kicks it away. He gets an identical ball out of his pocket, throws it in the air, bellows, serves fast and out. The skinny woman takes one step forward, waiting for the second serve, but he says "Ace!" says "Fifteen all," and goes back to his initial position. I saw the ball clearly fall a foot outside the line, but the skinny woman doesn't protest, just scratches her head and stands ready for the next delivery.

I climb up into the green, long-legged umpire's chair. I notice how a new course of bricks has doubled the height of the wall around the outside of the grounds. A bit more and the wall will blot out the tops of the trees in the forest. I don't doubt my brother-in-law will go on building up that wall until he's blocked out the mountain vista and the helicopter flight-path. When my sister gets back, the wind won't blow here any more, and the days will be much shorter. I stare at the wall, hear the ball popping on the synthetic surface, to and fro, backwards and forwards, my brother-in-law's voice more and more remote, and I feel I'm being gradually lifted up as if my chair was on a crane. Or perhaps my brother-in-law's sinking slowly into a crater, succumbing to an avalanche of tennis balls. I wake up when he throws his racquet to the ground and says "I can't concentrate like this." I didn't do anything, I was only thinking, but soon I see the butler was to blame, he had just come on court without asking permission.

The butler places the tray on a green table, and takes three wet glasses and a bottle of vodka covered

in a layer of ice out of a bucket. My brother-in-law
and the skinny woman walk to the base-line; he's
wiping a towel over his face and puffy neck. I get
down from the chair, as the gloved butler pours out
the drinks. When he turns to hand me my glass, he
displays a hematoma down the right side of his face,
from his temple to his jaw; around a depression of
yellowy skin there are three prominent arcs, russet,
purple and black-coloured, while the corner of his
mouth is a lump of congealed blood. As he takes the
empty tray out, the skinny woman says "Poor fellow." She downs her vodka in one gulp and shouts
"Hidrólio!" The butler stands there and says
"Madam," and the skinny woman "It wasn't anything really." "I thought Hidrólio had gone deaf,"
she says, but my brother-in-law explained it was his
sense of smell he lost. And that the doctor still
doesn't know whether the anosmia comes from being
hit by a gun-butt or from psychological trauma. The
skinny woman snaps her fingers, says "Oh!" and
goes off to rummage in her tennis bag, which I left
on the green-slatted bench. She brings over a toy
piano, the top of which she opens and sets off a
waltz. She takes out of the piano a tranquilliser
which she guarantees works wonders, telling my

brother-in-law to take it with vodka because it doubles the impact.

They drink one more glass and leave the court without saying anything, with him carrying both racquets and her bag. I follow them as far as the swimming-pool changing rooms, but they go into the sauna and slam the door quickly so the steam doesn't rush out. I go round the pool three times and return to the court. The bottle of vodka is half empty, I down a glass in one gulp. I walk round the court, my sneakers squelching on the green rubber surface. I retrieve the bottle and drink the vodka left straight from the neck. The profusion of yellow balls at the foot of the green wire fence reminds me of a flower bed. I pick them up one by one, think of making a game up. By the time I've picked a big armful the floodlights go out. I throw the balls up in the air and they are phosphorescent. For a moment I experience a kind of happiness, with the feeling I'm breathing in more air than I need.

As I leave the court, I bump into the table, knocking over the bucket and the bottle, shattering the wine glasses. I go in the changing room, switch on the light, slip into the sauna, closing the door quickly; but there's no steam left, and the water on the bricks is almost cold. On the seat there's a towel, a bottle of hair-conditioner, a disposable razor and a striped foam pillow. I spread the towel out, lie down, the pillow gurgles under my ear, and I think I'll go to sleep. I think I'm asleep when a servant in a turban appears at the door. Three Doberman puppies run through his legs and slide on their bellies over the tiles. The servant has got a mercurochrome stain on his bandaged head, he waves a rag and says dinner's on the table.

When I go in the dining room, I see my niece with a disfigured face. I sit down opposite her, and it's obvious she's been playing with her mother's make-up. She's got one green cheek, and one with a layer of blush-brown, and her lipstick-covered mouth looks like a tomato. She scrapes the prongs of her fork across her empty plate and the arm of the skinny woman at my side goes all goosepimply. The butler brings in a dish of roast grouper, which he serves French-style. After the skinny woman it's my turn, but I don't feel like eating fish. I search out some roast potatoes and half a spoonful of the manioc stuffing, but don't fancy anything. I have a glass

of white wine, and fear I've lost my sense of smell.
The kid goes back to scraping the enamel on the plate
and puts my teeth on edge. My brother-in-law serves
himself a thick slice of fish, then digs a tunnel into
the fish in search of more manioc. The butler takes
away the fish and comes back with a dish of rice.
The skinny woman tells him to leave the rice on the
table, that it's time he dealt with the kid, who's now
dragging her knife across the bottom of her plate.
The butler brings in a steaming tureen with no lid.
He fills the kid's plate up with ravioli in white sauce
and scatters parmesan cheese over the top. The kid
starts mashing the ravioli, which is stuffed with spin-
ach. She notices I'm looking at her, and lifts up her
plate with both hands as if to offer me the ravioli.
But suddenly she turns the plate upside down over
her own head and the béchamel drips over her make-
up. The nanny comes and carries the kid outside.

   The skinny woman crosses her knife and fork and
starts singing "Hmmmmmmmmmm," a strange
melody she must be making up right now. A wet curl
hangs down her forehead like a spring, and she's
wearing buttoned-up overalls with a hood at the
back. My brother-in-law, a bit of manioc in his
mouth, says he's had two exchanges with the girl's
psychologist. He was advised to talk openly to his

daughter, for even though she was asleep she took
in through some channel everything that happened
the night of the robbery. A silence descends while
the butler goes round the table filling up the wine
glasses. Then the skinny woman backs up the psychologist and says the kid needs to work out her
fantasies. My brother-in-law says "Shit," pushes his
plate away with some fish skin and bones, and says
even now he's got a taste of metal in his mouth. The
butler comes in with the trolley and takes the plates
away without stacking them. I think I'll take advantage of the pause to say goodbye, but the skinny
woman sits up on her chair and says "I've got it."
She opens her personal organiser and reminds us
that, with the time difference, my sister must be in
her hotel now. The butler brings the cordless phone
on a tray. My brother-in-law sends the butler out,
and says my sister needs to relax. I try to imagine
my sister in a foreign hotel room, but my brother-in-
law interrupts me to ask if I saw the bandits' faces
in the newspapers. I didn't see anything, but nod so
as to cut the conversation short. The skinny woman
says she was sorry for the youth, the one who looked
like a surfer. My brother-in-law says he was the
most dangerous one, because he was totally stoned.
The skinny woman can't accept that the surfer was

worse than the big black. My brother-in-law says that at least the black man was a professional, his hand wasn't shaking. The butler comes in with the dessert trolley, and the skinny woman sings "Hmmmmmmmmmmm." I think about my sister sitting on the edge of her bed in the hotel, perhaps downing her tranquilliser with a glass of port, and my brother-in-law asks if I read the story about the dollars that the newspapers put together. I nod, wanting to change the subject, and the skinny woman says the newspapers had to embroider the story, because there's no interest in saying the thieves left the house empty-handed. My brother-in-law says nobody keeps a million dollars at home, nor do people have a safe at home any more. The skinny woman hits her wooden backrest three times and says the next robbery they must welcome the thieves at the door with a million dollars. My brother-in-law agrees to this, so he would be spared spending another three hours with the barrel of a revolver in his mouth. And neither should my sister have to turn her closet upside down looking for her jewels like a madwoman, according to the skinny woman. Having said that, she nudges my arm. The butler comes in to pour the wine, and my brother-in-law notices her nudge me a second time. I act as if she wasn't with me, but she puts her hand on mine and asks if I prefer cinnamon or plum sorbet or a spoonful of each. My brother-in-law says the newspapers were decent about that and did respect my sister. I want to think about my distressed sister, walking slowly along the hotel corridor, but I can't recall her face now. My brother-in-law asks if I knew my sister offered to hand over all her jewels to the crooks, and I nod again. He says this didn't come out in the newspapers, but the skinny woman assures us it's the talk of the town. My brother-in-law asks if I knew the jewels had disappeared. I wipe my mouth with my napkin, as I see the residue of wet manioc on his lower lip. He asks whether I knew what the criminals did to my sister on the closet floor. In spite of the air-conditioning, my brother-in-law is sweating profusely on the top of his brow and down his neck, and his eyes are bulging. He says "Did you know?" repeats "Huh?" and waits for me to say "No," in order to satisfy his compulsive need to relate everything that they did to my sister on the closet floor. I nod, and the butler announces the arrival of the chief of police. The skinny woman orders the butler to serve coffee in the lounge.

TEN

Not for the first time my legs wobble when I get up suddenly. I take three silly steps before steadying myself, and the skinny woman laughs, thinking I'm drunk. I remember my father, who complained of limbs going to sleep, thought it was heart problems and had a monthly check-up. As we leave the dining room, the skinny woman in front and my brother-in-law just behind me, I dash into the bathroom. Whenever I need to urinate in a hurry, it always upsets me to take my prick out on the right, which is the wrong side, and which forces me to twist it round before it comes out. Finally I take aim at the centre of the bowl, my bladder's full, but the liquid's burning and reluctant to pour out. Something's inhibiting me. It's as if the hand holding my prick didn't belong to me. I get this feeling there's someone invisible next to me holding my prick. I shake that hand, articulate my fingers, change my grip, become aware of my hand, but now it's as if I was manipulating the prick of a stranger in front. I can't feel my bladder any more, I give in, zip up my fly.

The butler's waiting outside the bathroom to accompany me through the sitting rooms, along a corridor that's so wide it's a sitting room in itself. On the way there is a collection of odd-sized rugs, laid out asymmetrically on the wooden plank floor. I imagine an archipelago, and I'm forced to jump from one rug to another, sometimes with a clatter. Between the last rug and the marble floor of the main lounge, there's an ocean of wood I'm reluctant to walk on.

Although they can't see me, I know they sense my presence, because the lounge is silent. I think two acquaintances can exhaust a topic, four can eye one another and keep each other quiet for a while, but it's not natural for three creatures to stay silent in a room, on account of the very restlessness of the odd numbers. Finally the skinny woman coughs without really wanting to cough and my brother-in-law points his cup at me, saying "He's the one." The chief of police gets up sprightly, and seems to take off the upholstery, since his check jacket blends with the English cloth on the sofa. He comes over smiling, he's a young man, about five feet ten, his hair done up in a short pony-tail, is wearing jeans, chamois boots, and holds his hand out to me. I can't remember if I know him from television, newspaper photos or magazine covers, but I know he's someone famous; someone people meet and look at twice because the first time his skin seems false, and that's fame.

He greets me in a way he thinks informal, with an upturned hand, and leads me with his other hand on my back over to an armchair without arms. He settles down almost full-length on the sofa, his legs crossed on top of the coffee table. He picks up a glass of blue liqueur that he doesn't drink, and talks like someone dealing cards, considering each of us at regular intervals. Sometimes he also seems to be addressing a levitating interlocutor, which I discover is his image reflected in the tilting glass panels.

From what the chief of police says, I gather that

early one morning he drove up to the condominium, his siren blaring, came into the house, and found two guards and three dogs who'd been shot dead, a chauffeur in his death agony, plus two labourers with head wounds, smashed windows, walls and works of art scored by bullets, fresh blood on the big staircase, nanny clinging to child inside a room, the master bedroom turned upside down, the closet, my shell-shocked sister. After the ambulances arrived, he had a drink in the pantry with my stammering, pyjama-clad brother-in-law, and must have heard four times the story of what they did to my sister on the closet floor. I understand that early in the morning he assembled seven police to launch a raid on the shantytown crammed the other side of the woods, where he caught two criminal elements on the run, who offered no resistance and confessed they'd committed the assault. He searched the inside of their shack, apprehended a quantity of narcotics and an arsenal: hand grenades, automatic machine guns, pistols, shotguns, rifles for the exclusive use of the Armed Forces. In the meantime the delinquents tried to escape, but were mowed down at the foot of the hill by members of the police squad. The chief of police exhibited weapons and drugs at a press conference in the district he's head of, thus provoking an acid stomach in the deputy chief, who'd been longer in the service, whose kinky hair was going grey, who hated both film crews' lights and his superior's pony-tail.

After a buffet with some reporters in the canteen, the chief of police must have had a bath and a change of clothes in the flat where he probably lives by himself in the centre of the city. He got to my sister's house in the early afternoon, as he'd promised my brother-in-law, and found them having breakfast at the oval table in the winter garden. He opted for passion-fruit juice and listed the new security measures he would recommend to the couple, such as electrification of the walls, the periodic replacing of all domestic staff and the contracting of two bodyguards for each member of the family. My brother-in-law recorded these instructions on a Dictaphone and asked permission to leave to go to a meeting with his lawyers.

The chief of police doesn't say so, but I can almost swear my sister persuaded him to stay a little longer. She would be in a sleeveless dress and, as she invited him to walk round the garden, certainly realised the dark circles under her eyes would stand out

in the daylight and that a policeman would appreci-
ate women with dark circles under their eyes. As
they walked down the main garden path, she would
prudently refer to the jewels affair. I imagine the
chief detective said he'd already organised surveil-
lance of the fences or ordered the chambermaid's
lover to be investigated. Then she'd interrupt their
stroll, look him in the eye, and beg for the complaint
to be withdrawn please and the case to be closed.
The chief of police must have been disturbed less by
the woman wanting to protect someone than by
seeing her so vulnerable again, as if she were still
stretched out in her nightdress on the closet floor.

In the early evening the chief of police retired to
his flat, but I expect he didn't manage to sleep,
though he'd been up all night. He went back to my
sister's house after dinner on the pretext of testing
out the newly contracted night guards. He was wel-
comed by my brother-in-law in this same room, and
must have looked rather constrained on this English
sofa where he's lolling today. Avoiding asking after
my sister, he must have changed position every second, twisted his neck round whenever the butler
came in with the iced vodka or pastries. Enjoying the
scene and keen to prolong it, my brother-in-law no

doubt withheld news of my sister's untimely trip. And took the opportunity to talk leisurely about the farm his wife's family owns in the mountains. I reckon he gave such a detailed description of the farm even an amateur detective would see he'd never been there. But he wouldn't have forgotten to call it paradise, and to give its area and the value per square metre, before mentioning that the place is occupied by law-breakers. He showed his anxiety at the apparent impasse, taking account of the inactivity of the local authorities, the sluggish nature of the legal system, and the fall in property prices in the affected region. He admitted to experiencing momentary financial difficulties, and showed interest in getting rid of the property, still in the name of his wife's family, though it would be impossible as long as the abnormal situation obtained. As he showed the detective out, my brother-in-law was careful to tell him that his wife was flying abroad that evening, but would soon be back and left her regards.

Now the chief of police is telling us the situation on the farm in the mountains is more serious than he suspected. He informs my brother-in-law that he's got the file on the squatters. He tells the skinny woman they're people with powerful connections.

He finally says to me that tonight he personally is going to lead the investigation. He puts his glass of blue liqueur on the coffee table and gets up, uncrossing his legs, without leaning on the sofa. He says it's time to go, and kisses the skinny woman's hand, asking her to remain seated. He embraces my brother-in-law, who was already standing up, and tells him to expect an early-morning telephone call. He looks at the glass panel and says "Let's go?" giving the impression he's summoning his reflection to the investigation. But he quickly pulls me up out of the armchair, and, with one hand on my arm, and the other on my back, guides me through sitting rooms and gardens.

In the garage packed with wide sober cars, the yellow taxi is almost an arrogance. We get in, me in the back and the chief of police in front, on the right. The servant with the bandaged head is talking in the patio to a fellow in a shiny suit, whose hands in the distance seem to be holding up a big fish on display. This fellow gives a start when the chief's blast on the hooter echoes round the garage, and he hops over to us. He is in fact carrying an artificial leg, which he inserts through the window down on the seat next to me before getting into the driver's seat.

The car's an automatic, and instead of a meter there's a radio system with a microphone the detective talks into in order to broadcast our route. We drive down the hills in my sister's district, and the artificial leg rolls over to my side. I caress the artifact, which is made of a chestnut-brown plastic material, what they call flesh-coloured, though the owner's skin is somewhat darker. I think maybe it's a prosthesis he's rented, or hastily imported, or indeed perhaps preferred that way, after consulting the catalogue. There's a metal socket with fastenings just under where the knee should go, and I put my hand inside to see if the leg's hollow. The shoe's a traditional design, varnished and pointed-toed, and the silk stockings are glued to the shin.

We cross the city at a slow speed, and I notice other cars lining up behind us. Past the suburbs the driver speeds up, at the head of quite a long caravan. I move the leg over to behind the back seat, the bends round the foot of the mountains always make me sleepy. As it's a moonlit night, I can make out the banana trees proliferating up the hillsides and identify the camouflaged tents along the edge of planted land. I can see the chief of police's profile, but no longer hear what he's saying into the micro-

phone, and what the driver's giving the thumbs up
to. I imagine maybe he's crooning, and the radios in
the cars following us would pick up his voice. And
the people would go "Shhhh" in the cars, in order to
hear the recital better. And his singing should sound
intimate, his labials very present because the microphone's pressed against his mouth. And if I closed
my eyes, I would also hear the chief of police's song,
and be impressed by such a big man singing so
smoothly.

The taxi jolts over a speed bump, and reduces
speed. Sitting back up in my seat, I can see by the
side of the road a sign with a red arrow and the words
"Brialuz service station." We drive past the station,
which is deserted, and turn down a sandy road. The
dust diffuses the beam from the headlights, the at-
mosphere is that of a very misty midday. Human
shapes are following the slowly moving cars; we're
in a village, and its inhabitants must have got out of
bed to welcome the cortège. The cars park next to
each other, and they're private cars, in a variety of
makes. When the dust settles, the battery of headlights is aimed at a tiled façade, whose door and
windows look straight out on the road. The village
population gathers round, sensing something big's

about to break. But because there are so few of them
and so inexperienced in big things, they wander in a
huddle over the floodlit sand. And scatter when they
see four men jump from each car, men in suits but
not ties, whose faces escape me. Some have their
backs to me, or are wearing turned-up collars, sun-
glasses, or caps pulled over their heads. Others advance on the taxi and the power of the headlights
blots out their features. They make a human corridor
from the taxi to the tiled house, down which the chief
of police now walks, his hands in the pockets of his
check jacket. He slows down when the door opens,
and picks up speed when he can make out on the
doorstep an almost bald man in a jogging suit, em-
bracing a buxom woman in a yellow wig and brocade
dressing-gown. They say hello, go into the house and
close the door.

The driver gets out of the taxi, and asks me to
pass him the artificial leg. Leaning on the mudguard,
he rolls up the bottom of his shiny trousers and fits
the prosthesis to the stump of his left leg. The vil-
lagers regroup to get a close look at the operation,
and disappear when the door to the house opens
again. The chief of police comes out, his hand on the
shoulder of the man with the wispy hair, who has put

on a leather jacket and walks down the corridor of faceless men like a senator, smiling and nodding from side to side. He's led to the taxi and sits next to me on the back seat. The chief of police addresses him as a colleague, and introduces me as the owner of the farm, the injured party and citizen with a complaint. He grips my hand tightly, squeezing it for a good while, as though he were meeting me for the first time. But I recognise him from his ex-boxer's flat nose.

The taxi reverses, brakes, starts off as if going some distance and swerves in front of a house on the corner, twenty metres away. It's the local police station, and on the adjacent piece of ground is the old police van that's been visiting the farm. Chief of police and ex-boxer jump out of the car at the same time, and the driver twists round to open my door from the inside. The ex-boxer sits down behind the wheel of the van, and the chief of police signals to me to get in on the other side. I get in and settle down in the middle of the front seat, thinking the chief of police will prefer the window. But he doesn't get in; he slams the door and bids goodbye with two taps to the bonnet, like someone shooing a horse away.

ELEVEN

As he drives the van back to the road, the ex-boxer takes several deep breaths and makes half-gestures; apparently he's trying to tell me something grave, which only makes the ensuing silence graver still. We drive through the service station, and the other cars trailing us come halfway along the dirt track to the farm. I follow them in the rear-view mirror, and, when their headlights switch off, it feels stuffy in my seat. I want to open the window, but can't find the handle, and the ex-boxer's using up all my oxygen. He keeps changing gear, braking, and swerving as if he'd seen animals on the track. The van jolts so often I can't fix my mind on anything.

The gate opens as we approach, as if set off by remote control. The van stops, and the shaven-headed kid pops up with the three German shepherds, who sniff round the doors. The ex-boxer orders the kid to leave the gate open, get rid of the dogs and go down to the house. He's forced to repeat the order, because the kid stands rooted there, staring at me, until he swipes the air with a stick of bamboo and fades into the undergrowth with the dogs.

The twins in the striped shorts are waiting next to the trailers, probably alerted by the clattering van. They walk towards the moving vehicle, halt and turn round when they catch sight of me. The ex-boxer switches the engine off and puts it into first, but the van still hiccups down the bumpy slope. The twins position themselves by the bonnet, each carrying a club. They hesitate for a moment, bend down, then wedge the front wheels with the clubs. The ex-boxer jumps out and heads over to the biggest trailer, which is in darkness with its curtains closed. One of the twins opens my door and drags me out of the van. The other one supports me, pulls up my shirt and fondles my chest, plays with my nipples. I see the ex-boxer climb up the three steps and batter on the trailer door. The first twin twists my face round with both hands and sticks his little fingers in my ears, pressing hard, as if he wanted them to meet inside my skull. The second one separates us, puts me against a tree, where I think he's going to kiss my mouth, when there's a burst of machine-gun fire inside the trailer, and the ex-boxer flies back down the steps. The twins go over to help him, but he pulls himself together, dusts his leather jacket and says "Fucking shit." The door to the trailer half-opens and the redhead emerges naked, wearing so many rings and bracelets that he looks even more naked. He's clutching what appears to be a toy machine gun, not the size of his forearm. He's got a scar like an embroidered tie from Adam's apple to navel. His face is crumpled from sleeping and his left eye's covered with secretions, as if he'd woken up with conjunctivitis.

We all go into the trailer, the ex-boxer closing the door behind us. The redhead puts the machine gun down on the glass table, and goes into the bathroom at the back of the trailer. He turns the shower on, which reproduces the noise of a television that's switched down without a picture. The twins sit themselves on the edge of the divan with screwed-up sheets, opposite the snow on the television, and fight over the video tapes scattered on the rug. The ex-boxer sits back in the armchair by the table hefting the machine gun. I stand there against the door, counting the bullet holes on the ceiling.

The redhead comes out of the bathroom with hair rinsed, lucid eyes, a towel round his waist and a gold medal on his chest that highlights his coarse, keloidal scar. He sits down opposite the ex-boxer, smooths out the purple table cover and says "Where is it?" The ex-boxer says "Where's what?" "Where are the jewels?" says the redhead, looking at me out of the corner of his eye. The ex-boxer points the machine gun at me, and says he didn't take me seriously either, reckoned I was a pick-pocket, a petty thief, a waif and stray. And now he's discovered I own this farm. He quickly explains I'm not there to evict anyone, on the contrary, I've come with a proposal of interest to everyone. He takes a deep breath and says I introduced him earlier that evening to members of a big organisation, but the redhead's paying no attention to what he says; he gets up, goes round the table, stops in front of me without staring at me; his left eye is made of glass. He turns to the ex-boxer and says "You playing games with me?" his voice reaching falsetto in mid-sentence. The ex-boxer cringes in his armchair, and seems to masturbate the barrel of the machine gun. One twin turns the television off, the other draws the curtain, and the glaring headlights light up the pitted ceiling. The ex-boxer stands up and says "I took the liberty of inviting the guys from the organisation over for a chat"; his words came out firmly, in one breath, but as he finishes his sentence, he unconsciously hitches backwards. Not even a movement, a barely perceptible dorsal contraction, but enough to allow the redhead to step forward and force him back against the wall. An armed man has no right to retreat and, in this situation, brandishing a machine gun is but a theatrical gesture. He's now hemmed in, and could easily be pinned down by the twins, who nevertheless look in my direction and stand dead still. The redhead also looks through me and goes as pale as an albino. The chief of police has just come in behind me, leaning sideways so he can fit in the trailer. He doesn't even have to take his hands out of his

pockets for the three of them to put theirs behind
their heads. Nor does he have to open his mouth for
them to lower their eyes and walk out of the trailer
in single file, followed by the ex-boxer with the machine gun at the ready.

The chief of police sits down in the redhead's
chair and fingers the objects on the table. He opens
the tubes of medicine, sniffs them, empties a bottle
of sleeping pills on to the rug. He presses down at
random the digits on the turtle-shaped telephone and
leaves the shell upside down, rocking from side to
side. He holds up the porcelain Buddha, unscrews it
like a bulb, and the little figure's stomach opens up;
its belly is full of a white powder, probably cocaine.
We hear a rapid burst of gunfire outside, and the
chief of police says "The fools tried to escape." He
dips his finger in the cocaine and rubs it on his gums.
I'm going to peep out of the window, but he says
"Well, what a coincidence." He opens up a mother-
of-pearl box and asks if I'd recognise my sister's
jewels. Without waiting for a reply, he spreads the
jewels out on the table and says they fit exactly the
description my sister gave him. He distributes them
among the pockets of his check jacket, suddenly
stands up, hits his head on the ceiling and leaves the
trailer.

I didn't want to look, but there were the three bodies face down on the grass, side by side, hands crossed behind their heads. The chief of police walks down to the stream with the driver in the shiny suit, who barely drags his leg. The other men go on ahead, and are already crossing the plank bridge to the main farmhouse, where a light is flickering. The detective stops, turns round and beckons to me to go with him. I think these people have finished with the farm. I look straight at the chief of police and say "That's enough," but my voice goes so faint I can barely hear myself. Perhaps he hears, because he shakes his head and leaves my field of vision.

I go up in the opposite direction, and notice it's starting to get light on the top of the mountains. Near the gate I lean against the round stone where I liked to sit when I was little. I remember how at dusk I used to invite my sister to climb the stone and she always said "I'm coming," told me to go on ahead and sit down and wait for her. So I spent all night alone up there on top of it, having realised that night is superior to day. And that when dawn comes, it's not the day being born on the horizon, but night retiring into the bottom of the valley.

I cross through the gate, and hear a boom, which could be either thunder or shots echoing around the hillsides. It could even be both. Soon it starts to rain and the plantation catches fire.

I walked slowly along a good part of the dirt track, my head high, proud to feel the rain. I speed up when I notice it's morning. I throw off my muddy sneakers, which weigh me down. I run barefoot, slither a bit, and the rumbling that pursues me must be distant thunder. But it may also be the van, the taxi, the fleet of private cars; if they catch me up, they'll think I'm trying to escape. I stick my fingers in my ears the way the twin did, feeling the swollen cartilage. I run along with my eyes shut, I know the way. The puddles get deeper and deeper as I make amphibious progress. I finally tread firm ground, and see myself running at full tilt across the road in front of the Brialuz service station.

I recognise the skinny character in the check shirt at the stop for the bus that goes down the mountains. Seeing him there, I don't know why, fills me with feelings similar to gratitude. I keep on running towards him, my arms open wide, but he misreads me; he hunches his shoulders and pulls a knife out of his trousers. It's a rather rusty kitchen knife, its edge corroded, which he keeps pointed at my stomach, but I have no way of stopping my impetus. I'm a few inches from that long face, that gaping mouth, and I'm no longer sure I know him. Actually, I only know him from the check shirt, and it's the shirt I hold tight, and grab, and rip. I get the full length of the blade in my flesh, and almost ask the fellow to leave it there; I guess it'll hurt me more when it comes out than when it went in. He pushes my chest away in order to extract it, then disappears up the slope that leads off elsewhere.

As I get on the bus I remember I haven't got money for the fare. I pat myself in front of the bus driver, who looks at the bright stain on my shirt, makes a face and lets me in. I'm lucky to find an empty seat behind a fat black pop-eyed priest, and in front of a greeny-coloured individual who's sleeping with the right side of his face squashed against the window. The driver takes his time setting off; he looks around, apparently expecting other passengers. I consider telling him that today the kids with the limes won't be coming, but feel an immense weariness. I rest my head against the window.

Nor will they refuse me a telephone token at the bus station. I'll ring my mother, for I must lie down somewhere, have a bath, wash my hair. When my sister gets back from her trip, she'll willingly lend me six months' rent for a flat. If Mummy doesn't answer, I'll walk to my friend's house; he'll agree to put me up till my sister gets back. If my friend's dead, I'll knock at my ex-wife's door. She'll certainly be very busy, may even be embarrassed by the unexpected visit. She may open the door just a crack and wedge it with her foot. But when she sees the bright stain on my shirt, perhaps she'll make a face and let me in.